Butterfly Love:

the first flutter of a teen heart...

SeemaRaj

BlueRose ONE .com DIY
Stories Matter
NewDelhi • London

BLUEROSE PUBLISHERS
India | U.K.

For permissions requests or inquiries regarding this publication, please contact:

BLUEROSE PUBLISHERS
www.BlueRoseONE.com
info@bluerosepublishers.com
+91 8882 898 898
+4407342408967

ISBN: 978-93-7139-263-1

First Edition: June 2025

To

God who binds the world with love.

Raj, my soulmate, who always knows my strength more than me.

All the hearts that carry the fragrance of their first love forever!!

And finally, Chetan Bhagat—my inspiration!!

This book is a work of fiction. All the names, places, characters and incidents mentioned in this book are purely a product of the author's imagination or are used fictitiously. Any resemblance to actual places or persons, living or dead, events or locales are purely coincidental.

I am very grateful to the following people for helping and assisting me in their own many generous ways during the making of this book. Raj, Smitha, Anand,Shreya, Shreyas,Abhinand and Yashas.

Thank you and love you all !!

BUTTERFLY LOVE

June 1996: Madras Madness (Chennai)

Shakun

The orange rays of the setting sun seeped through Winny, a giant rectangular window designed with grilled iron bars of flower-shaped hexagons. She was a beautiful piece of constructive art on the first floor of the house, created by someone unknown. She had enough space for anyone to sit on her sides. She won the attention of every passerby who looked up to admire her beauty and size. Submissive to the hot touch of the April sun as much as she was to the chill rains of July, she stood proud, witnessing the lives of people in the neighbourhood. And her own home.
Winny was in a trance, admiring the fatigued sun fading away into its orange horizon, when Shakun came running and thumped on her lap in excitement. Winny looked at her and smiled. 'Ah! There she comes.'

Shakun held Winny's cool bars to her cheeks and whispered,

"Hello, Winny. Did you see him?"

Winny gazed at the girl who bestowed her the name, the foolish girl who conversed with a window as if it were a living entity. Shakun sat on her lap, looking up to the skies, dreaming the same dream that had always taken her away into the clouds, wondering if she could ever see the golden palace that was often there in her stories of right and wrong. Winny was her shoulder that carried her dreams of love and life. Shakun looked up and smiled at the blue sky, which had patches of white, wet cotton clouds sticking to it. Her 16-year-old smile had many new meanings that she was unaware of. Until recently, she realised that she had started to dream differently. This time it was not just a dream. It was real. She thought about Abel, her neighbour boy, who had become special from the moment she had seen him. She wondered why she had felt that surge of tender affection towards him. And now it was time for him to return from wherever he was. Her heart ached with a prayer. 'Oh God, bring him to me soon', when suddenly "Shakun..Shakun?" she heard her mother call. 'Urgh...amma...' she grunted as she quickly glanced down to the end of the narrow road, desperately hoping to catch a glimpse of Abel riding back home on his red bike.

"Enough dreaming. Come inside."

Shakun was the only child of her parents. Pampered but not spoiled. She was a typical, cheerful, confident girl, her hair curled up to her waist. Her curls were the pride that she genetically got from her mother. Shakun was much shorter and thinner for her age than all of her friends in the neighbourhood and school. People who saw her for the first time always assumed she would be just 12 or 13 years of age. She was petite, fair-skinned, quiet, and shy with round, transparent eyes that were more expressive than her words. A girl, mostly seen with a generous, hearty smile that had begun to draw attention from the boys around her. While other girls regularly carried sanitary napkins in their bags, Shakun had not yet attained her puberty. Her face had multiple acne spots that were showing out her signs of womanhood. But her petite personality was mostly a target for her friends to tease. Shakun would sometimes take it easy and at other times pretend to take it easy. Either way, her friends never saw the silent tears hidden in her eyes. That's Shakun, the star girl of our story.

1

One morning, amidst the early rush for school, with her eyes reaching out for her notebooks and lunch box that her mother had neatly packed, Shakun could hardly control her love thoughts for Abel, who had now taken a constant space in her heart. Like every day she hoped that Abel would step out for school at the same time as she did and they would clash with each other. She would get a chance to look into his eyes. She would allow him to see the shyness in her eyes, which would likely convey her confused feelings towards him. He would smile and offer to bike her to school. She would agree, sit behind him, and gently place her hand on his shoulder. He would then look at her through the mirror and smile shyly at her. Then life would turn magical. The same wish. The same hope. The same excitement. The same prayer.

Shakun hurried out of her door, and this time, her wish was granted. Abel emerged, twirling his bike keys in his fingers and whistling his beloved Michael Jackson song. 'I am bad. I am bad. You know it!' He was tall for a 17-year-old and looked most handsome in his perfectly pressed school uniform of a beige shirt and dark coffee-coloured trousers. His thin but muscled physique showed that he was regularly exercising. He combed his hair perfectly to the side and hung a brown backpack behind to match his uniform. He proudly pinned a bold red badge with the words 'Abel Alex, School Leader, 12A' to the right side of his shirt, just above the pocket. With a big round-faced black watch and neatly polished black shoes, Abel stood still, looking at her with the most perfect dimple-cheeked smile that made her feel so drawn towards him. Shakun stood staring into his marble brown eyes, completely locked in. Her dream was coming true. Her heart throbbed a million beats. It was finally happening. He was there, standing in front of her. She shook herself to the present and bent down. But she knew he was still looking at her. She slowly forced herself to glance at him. Abel had stopped whistling and was now gazing at her. She felt the chills in her navel. Was he going to ask her if she wanted to be dropped off at school? Abel slowly walked towards her, and Shakun suddenly wished her eyes did not tell the truth. Abel came close to her, looked into her eyes, and whispered,

“Shakun, button up your shirt. You have missed the top one!”.

It took a while for Shakun to shake herself from her dreams and register the words that her ears had taken in. She stood there, still blinking into his eyes. He quickly winked and moved backward, away from her. Abel could not stop laughing as he rode away on his bike, continuing to whistle. ‘I am baaad’.

‘What? No..no.’ This was never in her dreams—never! Shakun looked down at her shirt. Her top button was wide open, exposing her innerwear that had carefully cupped her still-growing breasts. She couldn't handle this embarrassment. She froze in shame and ran back to her room. She pressed her face into her pillow and screamed. ‘Yes, you are bad. You are bad, Abel. I know it. I know it NOW!’

2

It had been a week since Shakun sat near her window. She did not wish to face Abel again. She now had only hatred for him. She despised him, not only for making her feel embarrassed but also for destroying her first sprout of tender love that had bloomed within and given her many moments of blissful shivers. He had trampled upon those pleasant dreams of her handsome prince riding on a horse to carry her far away into the woods. He had dropped her flat on the grounds of this real world of meanness and mockery. She could neither forgive nor forget him for that. Until one morning, Amma called out. 'Shakun! Jessy is here.'

Jessy was Abel's sister, but they shared no common physical features that could make them look like siblings. Jessy was excessively large and obese, with protruding breasts and rounded hips. Though just a year younger than Abel, Jessy was more mature and understood life much beyond her age. She enjoyed spying on people's intentions and behaviours, and she would get excited to share her discoveries with Shakun. This time, she felt the same excitement. Jessy barged into her room and closed the door behind her. The noise shook Shakun, causing her to turn around and look into Jessy's beaming eyes and broad smile, which instantly told her something amazing had hit her mind. Jessy hurriedly sat on the edge of Shakun's bed and swallowed hard. Shakun scanned her face for a clue and asked,

"What's up, Jessy?" You look excited.

“I have news, Shakun... I have solid news! You will not believe what I have to share.”

“News? What news?”

"It's about my stupid brother. I discovered something about him that I could blackmail him with." Jessy winked and side smiled naughtily.

"Blackmail? That happens only in movies, right?"

"Ohhoo...stupid… Do you want to know the news or not?"

"Eh..? Of course...can't wait." she lied.

Jessy came closer and whispered into Shakun's ears,

"Abel has a girlfriend. John told me. In fact, John took a promise from me to keep it a secret!"

Shakun felt her heart would stop beating. Could it be her? Did Abel tell John about his love for her? Was Jessy excited about the possibility of becoming sisters-in-law one day? The thought itself brought her back to the wet cotton clouds in her blue sky. She beamed an impulsive smile at herself. No. No. It's too good to be true. No, it can't be her. No, it is somebody else. Definitely. Though she thought she despised Abel, she could not accept anyone else loving him either. A sudden gush of love erased all her hatred for Abel, a love she could never truly let go of. Just like her first feeling of love, she now felt her first blow of jealousy towards someone she didn't even know yet.

She stared at Jessy, wondering if she had heard the screaming words in her head. 'No way... No way... I won't believe it. Abel cannot love anyone else... because he is mine.' But instead her mouth muttered the words.

"Oh...really? That's so sweet, isn't it?"

“Sweet? Are you mad? You wouldn't say so if you knew who the girl is.’

Shakun’s head screamed again. ‘I don't care who she is. Nobody can love Abel the way I do!’

“Oh..why? Who is it?” Shakun spoke, showing the least interest.

“It's KAVYA!” Jessy screamed with her hands open wide.

Kavya was Abel's classmate and also the most popular girl in school.

“Whaaaattt… Kavya? That nerd?.” Shakun yelled, while her heart burst with envy.

“Yeah. Also the most beautiful, I should say! Of all the boys drooling for her, she chose my brother. And why not? He is the most handsome, and he is also the school leader this year. But the sad part is that John saw them kissing yesterday in the backstage of our assembly hall. Poor John. He had gone looking for her to tell her how much he loved her, but saw this instead. Imagine..so sad,right?”

“What!!… Abel loves Kavya? And John loves her too?” Shakun felt her head would burst.

“But that's crazy. John never told me about his feelings for Kavya! Anyone observing Kavya with John would undoubtedly conclude that she loves him. Her jumpy 'good morning' hugs and flying kiss byes...and what not...how can it be? Are you sure, Jessy?” shrieked Shakun.

"Oh ho...calm down, freak! You think I am imagining it all? John himself told me about it. The poor fellow sounded so low and broken."

"So sad!" Shakun sighed and looked away from Jessy. She walked towards her mirror and saw a loser with a broken heart. Tears of both anger and sadness filled her eyes. Angry with herself for not being born as pretty as Kavya, angry with John for having kept his love, a secret from her. She was even more disheartened by the fact that both of their hearts were shattered at the same time.

She felt her head burn with the shock of the news Jessy had just shared. She could not even, for a moment, picture Abel and Kavya together, let alone them kissing. She could feel her heart bleed with despair. A sudden wave of loneliness engulfed her. She felt betrayed by Abel even before feeling his love. Abel had broken her heart once again, but this time forever. Shakun wished that someone would wake her up from this bad dream and bring back all her lost hopes of love that was meant for her. She kept waiting, but no one came. She stared at Jessy. 'Was she here to wake her up from this dream?' she asked herself. No.. Jessy was still sitting in front of her, and her lips were miming something that seemed important. But Shakun could no longer hear Jessy's words, as the noise in her head was much louder. She suddenly felt everything in the room move around in slow motion. She was caught between the sorrow of losing Abel and the bitter anger of losing him to Kavya, the only girl she had always hated since she had seen her. Shakun thought of John, and a new wave of anger ignited within her. 'The idiot never told me.' But she quickly realised that it was probably not the right time for her to be angry, and instead she needed to understand his grief. It struck her that John was also probably feeling as sad and neglected as her. Her empathy for John reminded her of the special place of brotherhood that she had for him in her heart. It had been only a month since Shakun and her parents moved from Madurai to this house in Madras. Since then, John has always been her FAB—her Friend and Brother.

3

May 1st, 1996: Madurai to Madras

It was a scorching day in Madras, when they had finally reached their new home.

Robert, the house owner, smiled.

“It's not as merciful as Madurai. The heat here will suck out every drop of sweat from your insides,” he laughed. “Hope your trip was fine. Where is your load truck?”

“We had a safe journey. Thank you.” Mr. Das, Shakun's father said, smiling. "The truck will reach by evening." Amma joined her hands for a vanakkam (namaste) for Mr. Robert.

“Ammu... come here, dear,” she called out, looking towards the taxi.

Shakun peeped out of the taxi, still confused about why they had to leave behind a calm, peaceful city like Madurai for this new, loud, and crowded metro. She was still too young to understand the compulsions of life that had forced her parents to take such a permanent decision unwillingly. She knew she missed her hometown friends and wondered if they were also missing her. Though her parents looked happy, she clearly was not. Shakun never wanted to leave her Madurai home. It was her favourite Mad-town.

But now she was here. The matchbox houses, which adhered to each other with shared walls, completely captivated her. As she got out of the car and walked towards her parents, she wondered which of these matchboxes would become her home. It was not until she heard her father talk that she noticed Mr. Robert. Shakun gazed at the large, dark man with a protruding stomach, who was now grinning at her. His white teeth made his skin appear even darker, and she felt her first fear for him. Robert smiled and bent down to talk to her.

“Hello, paapa. (little one). Un per enna..what is your name?” He said it in a childish tone pinching her cheek.

She could smell chicken curry from his fingers, which she pushed away. She hated herself for being short; that made people think she was a child. She looked straight at him and said

“Shakuntala…”

“Oh..and they call you Ammu?” He asked, pointing at her parents.

“Yes, and sometimes, Shakun,” she said with pride.

“But what do you like?” he continued in his childish tone.

She said in a husky voice, "Shakun. I like Shakun."

“Okay, Shakun,” smiled the stranger.

Just when Shakun started to relax with Mr. Robert, she heard a scream of excitement from behind him. It was a boy's voice of victory. Shakun tilted her head sideways from Mr. Robert’s tummy and saw him. He looked a little older than her. He stood there, panting breathlessly and smiling wide with triumph, holding the legs of a wailing hen hanging upside down. Shakun's eyes opened wide.

"'Daddy, look, I caught her. It was a tough race to win," the boy yelled.

Mr. Robert turned and patted the boy's shoulder.

"Well done, John. I know you will bring her back." laughed Robert, and so did Shakun's parents.

"Come and meet our new tenants. And this is Shakun,' pointing down.

"This is John, my courageous son. He is 17 and already behaves like an adult," he laughed.

"Vanakkam uncle, aunty! Daddy had told me to buy some milk and today's newspaper for you. I've kept it near the window." he said in his responsible tone.

"Oh..really? That's very kind of you, young man. Thank you". Mr. Das said, tapping John's cheek.

"Come. Let me walk you both in, Mr. Das,"' said Robert to his new neighbour.

"Daddy, wait. Take her." John carefully handed the bird over to his dad, who continued to laugh with pride. The boy turned and walked toward Shakun. He was significantly taller, thin, and dark, with feather-soft, overgrown hair that required a push back, to reveal his eyes. He wore a white shirt and blue shorts, and he smelt the same as his dad's pinching fingers. Shakun stepped backward, unable to judge his next move. She searched for her parents, who were already walking away with Mr. Robert. John abruptly extended his hand, eager for a handshake, and spoke

"hello...sister. I am John. I know that your name is Shakun."

Shakun felt her anxiety fade away when she heard the word sister from John's mouth.

Shakun smiled and returned his handshake half-heartedly because she did not wish her hands to smell like his.

John smiled.

“Which school are you joining?”

“I don’t know. Appa said he will try to get admission for me into any of the nearby schools."

“How old are you? Which class will you get into?”

“I am 16. I will be in 11th now.” She spoke, sounding like a woman.

“What? 16? I thought you would be just 12 or 13,” he said and laughed.

Shakun looked down in silence. John realised his mistake and said

“Sorry. I did not say that to tease you.”

“It’s ok,” she said, feeling better with his apology.

“Mm... 11th, eh? That means you and Jessy are the same age.”

“Jessy?” Shakun blinked. She felt the name was a little funny.

“Yes. She is my best friend’s sister. You can meet her in the evening. I'll take you to meet my other friends, too. Okay?”

Shakun just shook her head in agreement, smiled shyly, and turned away to join her parents.

"Bye, sister," shouted John, waving at her.

Shakun felt new excitement grow inside her. She had become John's sister, which meant that he would take care of her like brothers normally do. She smiled and waved back.

She held on to her mother as she climbed up the stairs to their first-floor home. A square-shaped open space with a floor painted with red-oxide, stretched like a sit-out, from the stairs to their main door. On one side of this sit-out, facing the main door, was a huge window that caught Shakun's eye. It was massive, and filled the entire wall. Shakun stared at the window and felt it call to her. 'Hello Shakun...come! Sit on my lap and I will take you to your dreams.'

4

Present day: The Teen Tension

Jessy snapped her fingers at Shakun's face to bring her back to the present moment.

“Are you listening or not?” growled Jessy.

“Yes, yes..you were saying how sad it is for John. I agree.”

“What? No. I told you that John has become silent and needs help. Of course you weren't listening.”

“Oh, sorry, I missed that. Let's go and make him smile.”

They both ran down the steps and bashed into John’s house. John was at the kitchen dining table, helping his mom pull out the feathers of their freshly butchered chicken. Shakun felt her bile rise up to her throat when she saw the head of the bird hanging down the edge of the table and its blood oozing down to touch John's feet.

“Aunty... biryani for lunch?” chirped Jessy.

John's mother looked up and gave her an agreeing smile.

“Hello aunty.” Shakun waved at her.

She observed that John did not even look at them. Being in love with Kavya had kept his face glowing till then. But now he looked pale and lonely. She felt the urge to hug him and tell him that she too feels the same pain as his and that the pain of losing the hope of love is most dreadful in this world. She wanted to scream into his ears that she too feels cheated and undeserving like him. She wanted to tell him that she loved Abel as much as he loved Kavya. She wanted to...

However, Shakun remained speechless, like a silent nightingale. Her heart ached for herself and her beloved John. She had to do something to shake him out of that grief.

Shakun slowly walked towards John and sat close to him.

“To me, that dead chicken and you look the same. One dead from outside and the other from within.” She whispered into his ears.

John glanced at Shakun, pretending to search for the reason she said that.

“What?” John said

“I know John. I know how you feel.” she whispered

“You know nothing. You will never know. At least not yet. You won't understand," John replied with a manly tone.

“Hello!” she mocked. “I am just a year younger than you. Why would I not understand, eh?” Shakun rolled her eyes at John and squeaked.

“Ok..ok..sorry..aaaunty!” John teased to make her smile.

Shakun decided to tell John about her feelings for Abel. After all, it had been a while since she felt this crazy about Abel. She checked on Jessy, who seemed to be busy chatting with John's mother about how she had once helped her mom cook mutton. It was a wonder how a dead chicken could carry her away from John’s real world of deceit to her world of delicacies. Nothing was more joyful for Jessy than a plateful of her favourite food and nobody to share it with.

"I know it all, John, because..." Shakun looked back at John and blurted out in a hurry.

"Because?" John repeated

"Because I think I love Abel the same way as you love Kavya." Shakun said softly, gasping with relief that she had finally revealed the most terrifying secret she had ever kept to herself.

John cupped Shakun's mouth with his bloody palm and looked towards his mom and Jessy. But they were so much in love with a dead chicken than to hear Shakun's words. He stood up and washed his hands and Shakun's cheek, which was smeared with chicken blood from his fingers. He dragged her out of the kitchen and ran to the terrace, which was one floor above Shakun's house and now the only place for privacy.

"What the hell are you telling me, Shakun?" John shrieked, shutting the terrace door behind them. John held Shakun by her shoulder and continued. "You love Abel? You small girl!! Do you even know what love is?" John could not stop his words from spilling out. He did not understand how his younger sister could fall in love—it's not possible.

John stared at Shakun with anger and confusion until he saw the thin layer of tears filling her eyes.

"Stop calling me a small girl just because I am small in size, fab!" Shakun was frustrated now. "Maybe I don't know what love is. But I know that I want to be with Abel all the time. I know that I want to sit behind him on his bike and ride away with him. I know I want to hold his hand forever... I know that I felt my heart ache when I heard about Abel and Kavya being together. I know all this for sure. Now you tell me. Am I in love?"

John slowly loosened his grip on Shakun's shoulder and smiled. Shakun sensed that John was ready to joke about her feelings and disregard her as a confused girl wishing to grow up faster against nature's will. But instead...

"I can't believe my sister has grown to love." John whispered excitedly."Yes, you are, Shakun. You ARE in love!" John exclaimed with open arms and laughed out loud. After all, his father had proudly told him he was way too mature for a boy. And now this matured boy knows everything about love too.

Shakun was surprisingly scared by John's confirmation of her feelings for Abel. Her heart suddenly felt heavier. She had indeed experienced LOVE!! Finally, she felt sure. She felt certain because FAB had told her that it was love and so it should be. She felt her feet rise above the ground. She was flying into the rainbow coloured clouds, where Abel was waiting in his golden chariot. Shakun wished that the moment lasted longer, when John shook her back to reality with the scorching sun burning their feet and the aroma of chicken biriyani storming into their nostrils through the chimney tower.

"John… I am scared," blurted Shakun with lips that now shivered in the heat.

"Awww, my little one! Don't worry. I am here with you. What are brothers for otherwise?" John tapped her shoulders with the assurance of a brother's protection. Shakun smiled vaguely.

“But why did you not tell me about your love for Kavya? Why did you keep it a secret from me? I thought we were besties." Shakun complained.

“Yes, we are, and I am sorry that I never told you. In fact, I did not want to tell Jessy either, but I had to because she caught me running out of our assembly hall today, and I could not hide it anymore. I was in utter shock.” John admitted.

Shakun looked at John sadly.

“We both lost our first love," she said. “I feel sad for you more than myself, John. I wish Kavya and you were together.”

“I wish Abel for you too," whispered John as he wiped the tears off her cheek and sniffed the hunger-driving smell of Biriyani once again.

“Let's forget them now and have some juicy chicken legs,” he said, winking.

“Ewwww....me? Chicken? Noooo.... I will go home. Nothing tastes as delicious as my mom's drumstick sambar.”

“That's so boring, small girl.” John laughed and ran down the steps.

“Stop calling me small. I told you I hate that, FAB.” Shakun pushed John, but he dodged her.

“Really? But that's precisely what you are—a small girl.” John laughed and ran down faster, with Shakun right behind to catch him.

5

It was a clear night, a month after that heartbreaking day for John and Shakun, when they shared the pain of their hopeless love with each other. Now it seemed like John had already forgotten about it. Shakun sat by Winny's side and wondered how it was possible for him to just bury his love for Kavya so quickly while she, on the other hand, had not even come to terms with Abel and Kavya being together. She remained in a state of desperation, yearning for a magician who had been observing her struggles to suddenly intervene and transform her life. Even though she had stopped discussing Abel with John, she remained in despair and clung to the hope that Abel might return to her. She sat at her window and looked at the night sky. There were no cotton clouds this time. There was a vast expanse of blue, adorned with glittering stars. It was beautiful but looked empty without its clouds. Perhaps the clouds also abandoned the sky forever, she thought. For her, no clouds meant no golden chariot, no Abel! Shakun felt as empty as the sky. Tears rolled down. She pressed her cheeks against her window pane. It felt cold on her skin. She felt it hug her back. Her Winny knew it all. She looked at it and held the hexagons close to her face. She felt it say something. Just then, a tender, cool breeze swept through and blew away her tears. Shakun sensed a sudden calmness inside her. Something told her everything would be alright. Just when she smiled and kissed her window pane, she heard her mom call from the kitchen.

“Ammu ..? Ulle vaa (come inside)... It's dinner time!”

Shakun wiped the wetness off her cheeks with her sleeves and joined her parents. Appa was assisting Amma in setting the table, a task underlined in the home chore list that Amma had made for him. As Shakun sat down at her dining place, her eyes followed her mother's body movements, and she observed how slim and curvy she had always been. Shakun always loved her mom's physical features. An average 5.2-foot tall woman was mostly draped in light-shaded sarees that exposed her waist's curves. She walked with haste, her long, untrimmed plaited hair fluttering off her buttocks, her spectacles magnifying her eyes beyond reality, and her unwavering smile. Shakun admired her mother not just for her features but also for the 4-'H' values of life that she was very strict about: "To be Honest, Hard-working, Healthy, and Happy". As simple as that.

Shakun watched her father carefully carry the bowl of Dal, remembering how caring he had always been about her. Shakun was Appa's favourite girl, and he often introduced her to his friends with a lot of pride. He was too tall for Shakun's mother, who appeared smaller near him. When they stood together, people often teased them to look like the Bollywood famous couple, Big B and JB, which they found amusing. And now as they ate, Shakun mindlessly asked her father,

"Appa, how did you and Amma get married? Did you know each other before marriage?"

"Aye... What are you asking?" Amma interrupted. Appa swiftly grasped her palm and shook his head miming her to stop.

"What's wrong with that question?"

He turned to Shakun and smiled.

"Those days were different, dear. We don't get to see the girl until after the wedding."

“What?..really? Then how did you agree to the marriage, Appa?”

“That's a sad story.” Appa winked at Amma.

“Sad story? What happened? Please tell me.” Shakun pleaded.

“It’s a secret. Come closer.”

“Oh, come on.” Amma punched his shoulder and hinted at him to stop. But he continued.

“The day I went to her house with your grandparents, there were only men around. Her father, uncles, and nephews. Those days, women were not allowed to sit with men for any discussions or celebrations. When I learnt that the family elders would fix the proposal and that it was against our custom to see the girl before the wedding, I felt deeply disappointed. All the ladies were peeping out of the first-floor windows. Then, from one of the windows, I saw a beautiful smiling face who quickly turned away when our eyes met. I felt elated and agreed to the marriage, assuming she was my girl. But on the wedding day, in the mandapam, your mother came and sat next to me. I was so shocked. Everything happened so fast that I just had to accept her.”

“Oh my God... really Appa? Then what happened? Who was the girl at the window?”

“Aah, she happened to be one of your mother’s friends who was already married,” laughed Appa.

“Awww! That’s truly sad, Appa! But Amma is beautiful too.”

“Of course..” Appa glanced at Amma. "She has the most loving heart, and I am glad I agreed for the marriage, though it came in as a surprise package.” Appa chuckled while Amma and Shakun laughed together.

“You both are the best parents in this world,” announced Shakun with a loud cheer. ‘I would be the best wife for Abel, and we will be the best parents for our children,’ she thought and giggled. But instantly her heart pulled out the picture of Abel and Kavya kissing each other and placed it back in front of her eyes.

Shakun’s heart broke and bled like a tsunami all over her body, mind, and soul. She looked down at her plate. She was not smiling anymore, and not a morsel of food had been touched. Amma shook her out of her hurtful thoughts.

“Ammu..what is wrong? Why are you not eating?” She sounded frustrated this time.

Shakun could not hold on to her pain anymore, and she ran to her room, leaving her worried parents behind.

Back into her privacy, Shakun stared at herself in the mirror. She saw a weak, helpless, self-praising loser who had accepted defeat and given up on her love. ‘Your love is fake, Shakun. You're only 16. You don’t know what love is. You've never actually loved Abel. If you did, you would never let go of him as easily. You never loved him...NEVER!!!’ her mirror yelled at her.

‘THAT’S NOT TRUE,’ she screamed back. ‘John told me that it was love...yes, it was...and it is.’

Shakun's innocence confused her. Tears rolled down her cheeks. She covered her face with her palms and sobbed heartily.

Her outcry made her stronger, and she suddenly felt the urge to fight for her love and for herself. 'I will not let go of Abel. I'll get him back.' She gave the mirror a thumbs-up.

"Shakun... Are you okay? Open the door, dear!" Amma knocked.

Shakun quickly wiped her tears, let out a loud sigh, and opened the door with a painted smile.

Amma stared at her, questioning her with suspicion.

"What happened? Why did you run away like that? Wait, were you crying?"

"Uff..ma... So many questions. I just wanted to use the bathroom. That's all"

"Are you sure? You can always tell me anything without hesitation. You know that, right?"

"Yes. I know, Amma. And I will. Don't worry." Shakun lied.

They exchanged a friendly glance, and both went back to finish their meal.

6

That night Shakun stayed awake for a long time, thinking about the same thoughts that had popped up during dinner. 'Was Abel really my first love? Is this the love that Appa and Amma have for each other? Oh, God! Please help me understand.' The questions continued to haunt her until tears glued her eyes shut and carried her to an unknown land of familiar faces. The place seemed like a party house. She swept through the laughter-dancing crowd, eagerly searching for someone. There was Jessy filling her mouth with cream pie, her Amma waving at her, Appa smiling, and John holding a bleeding chicken head in his hand and jumping. All her school friends were giggling around her, but her eyes were searching for the most handsome face, which was nowhere in sight. She ran around screaming 'Abel...Abel...' but no one seemed to hear her or help her find him. Her fatigued legs made her drop down to the centre of the hall, and she wailed her heart out with the fear of losing him. She cried loudly in despair, but Abel was nowhere near her. Somebody in the crowd screamed excitedly,

"Let's welcome the new lovely couple, Abel and Kavya." Shakun lifted her head to see Abel, dressed in a wedding suit with tie and trousers, holding Kavya's hand. Kavya, dressed as a bride in a long white frilled gown and her hair beautifully braided with white pearls, was also extravagant. She looked very beautiful and proud in her bridal wear. Slowly, they walked towards Shakun, who was still on the floor. They bent down and laughed at her loudly. Their laughter got louder and louder, and slowly the whole crowd started to laugh, pointing at her. Shakun shut her ears with her hands and cried when suddenly she heard someone say, 'Abel is gone, Shakun... gone forever.'

That moment of loneliness shook Shakun out of her dreams, and she popped her eyes open. She stared at the fan above, taking a minute to understand what had just happened. It was a dream that God intended for her to witness and experience the agony of living without Abel. Shakun felt devastated, thrown to another planet without Abel. She felt like a dead leaf fallen and stamped into the dirt forever, like a lost child searching for the mother. Shakun felt weak, helpless, and sad. No, she could not imagine a life without him. Never. Not even in her dreams.

She could no longer get back to sleep. She opened the main door and slowly walked to her favourite place. She sat on her best friend, Winny's lap. She sat with her back resting on the side wall, leaning her head on the pane. She glanced up at the sky and saw the white moon smiling at her. "No moonie...not now.." She turned away with a frown. The silent world outside reminded her of her dream. Her cheek touched Winny's cold metal, and she hugged her tightly against her face. Tears rolled down and dropped on the sides of Winny's lap. 'I really love Abel, Winny. What do I do now? You tell me. You are the only one who knows everything. Please tell me...tell me, Winny.' And she sobbed until her tired eyes closed with despair. 'Go tell him, Shakun. Tell him how much you care. Just tell him. Just like that.' Shakun heard a voice and woke up. She looked around but found no one. She noticed that her hands had remained tightly gripped around Winny. 'Did you talk to me, Winny? Yes, you did. I heard it.' Shakun spoke excitedly. She suddenly felt clear about what she needed to do to help herself. 'Yes. I should just tell him. How would he even know otherwise? Yes! I will tell him. Tomorrow!' Shakun felt impulsive about it. She kissed Winny hard and felt the chillness of the metal on her tender lips. She smiled and looked at the sky. The moon was still there, looking sad. 'I am sorry, Moonie. Don't be mad at me,' she pleaded with folded hands, throwing a flying kiss at it. She felt cheerful and enjoyed the breeze that blew her hair with the fragrance of baby jasmines waiting to bloom. She felt refreshed and ready to open up face-to-face with Abel the next day. She was determined to be bold this time, unlike a month ago, on that marked day of her life when she met him and Jessy for the first time.

7

The New Kid in Town

She had just met John, who told her that he would take her to meet his best friends in the neighborhood. It was almost sunset when John came up to meet his new little sister.

"Hello Aunty, where is Shakun?" John asked Amma, who was lighting the diya, for her prayers.

"In her room, arranging her stuff." Amma smiled, pointing her fingers to the left.

"Can she come to meet my friends?" John was excited.

"Yes, yes...of course. She is sad and misses her hometown. If she makes friends here, she will feel better. Thank you, John."

"Shakun, John is here to take you. Come out." Amma called for her loudly.

Shakun came out quickly and smiled at John.

"Hello," she said meekly.

"Come..let's go."

Shakun walked with John to the end of the street, where she saw a group of boys. Two of them were fighting with each other. A boy in a red shirt, who was likely John's age, sat on top of another boy in yellow, who was lying on the ground. The boy in red was slapping him left and right. Suddenly, the yellow shirt pushed the red shirt, causing him to fall backward and hit his head on a large pile of red bricks that had been laid out for some construction work. The force of the blow tore his forehead, causing him to start bleeding. John, seeing this, ran towards them and joined the others who had been trying to stop the fight. John helped the boy in the red shirt stand up, while the others attempted to calm the boy in yellow. Shakun was shocked to see such a physical brawl, like in the movies. She saw John helping his friend walk towards a public pump to wash his bleeding wound. While she stood lost in the crowd, she felt a hand on her shoulder. Shakun turned to see a fat, pretty, chubby-cheeked girl smiling at her, with a lollipop in her mouth. Shakun observed the pink candy juice drooling along the sides of the girl's mouth as she smiled.

"Don't get scared. This happens almost every day. Did you see that boy in the red shirt? The one who got hurt in his forehead? That's my brother Abel. The yellow shirt is Murli." She spoke in a casual tone while licking her lollipop. "You are Shakun, right? John had told me that you would come," she cheered, pointing her index finger at Shakun.

"Yes." Shakun replied without a smile. She was still trembling in fear with what she had witnessed a few minutes ago.

"I am Jessy. Your neighbour. My house is just opposite to yours. I saw you and your parents coming in a taxi today."

"Why were they fighting?" Shakun asked in a meek voice.

"Ohooo... You are still thinking of that!" Jessy tapped her forehead.

"What was your first thought when you saw me, Shakun?" Jessy asked.

"What? Why?" Shakun asked back.

"Just tell me. How do I look? Be honest,ok?"

“My first thought? Honestly, you are fat. But I like your chubby cheek and your smile.” She quickly added to hide her first comment.

“It’s ok. You thought I was fat, right? That is the same reason my brother hit Murli. But Murli did not just think. He said it out loud. He laughed at me and teased me for having these big breasts. He called me a ‘gundu kozhi’ (fat chick). That’s all.”

Shakun’s eyes rounded in surprise.

“He is my big brother, Shakun. He loves and cares too much for me, and he gets angry if anybody teases or hurts me in any way.” Jessy sighed and continued.

“I know I am fat, but I don’t care. My mom always says that I am only 16 and will lose weight as I grow older. So I am not worried. But Abel…! He's a stupid boy. He takes everything seriously, gets angry and fights with everyone who even utters my name.” Jessy’s simple talk calmed Shakun and made her smile. For a moment, she wished she had a brother of her own who would care for her so much.

“You look like a ghost with all that blood. Mamma will definitely get worried.” Jessy remarked at Abel when she saw him walking towards them with John by his side.

“Shut up! Where are the others?” He asked Jessy.

“They all left as soon as they saw you bleeding. Nobody stayed to help you, my dear brother. They are not good friends.” She teased.

‘You want a whack from me? idiot!". Abel raised his palm but stopped when his eyes fell on Shakun.

“Who is this new face?” He looked sharply at Shakun.

“This is Shakun. I told you about... our new tenant.” John introduced.

Shakun looked at Abel and instantly felt her eyes stuck to his face. A wheat-skinned boy, slimmer and taller than John, who possessed the most captivating brown eyes and thick eyebrows that seemed to shield them from the world's grim and perilous visions. His oval-shaped face was perfectly sculpted, with a nose that shaped like the letter L. The blood stains from his wound had turned his red, pimpled cheeks into darker hues. Between his nose and mouth, there were brownish baby strands of moustache hair that looked shiny and new. A subtle cool breeze blew his thick, soft, bouncy hair to one side of his scalp. He shuffled his hair away from his forehead and smiled at her. His smile exposed his neatly arranged teeth and gave a quick deep dimple on his right cheek. Abel was the most handsome boy she had ever seen till now. Shakun felt a small bubble of attraction burst in her tummy, and for the first time in her life, she felt her tiny heart flutter like the wings of a butterfly.

Abel noticed Shakun lost in her thoughts. He bent down a little with his hands on his knees, came closer to Shakun's face, and spoke in a whisper.

“Hello. Dream Girl! “

Shakun was shaken from her bliss. She looked back closer into his brownish round marble eyes and nervously smiled sideways. She once again became conscious of her small physique.

“Hello,” she whispered.

“So you are Shakun, the new kid in town, eh?” Abel continued in a whisper.

Shakun did not like him calling her a kid. She wished she was taller. At least for him.

“John told me that you are the same age as my sister. Have your parents found a school for you?”

“Appa mentioned a school. I don’t remember.” She replied softly without blinking.

Shakun seemed to have forgotten everything about her life. Something was beginning to change inside her.

“It's ok. Little one.” Abel spoke in a pampering tone and laughed.

Shakun did not like him teasing her, but something about him made her feel that she would be okay with anything he says.

“Tell your dad to give our school a try. Little Hearts Higher Secondary. It's both the best and the closest.”

“Yes, yes. You and I can be in the same class. It would be so much fun!!” Jessy shrugged from behind with excitement.

“Fun to finish her lunch box too, eh?” Abel affectionately embraced his food-loving sister.

“Ha ha! Very funny. Let’s go home. Mummy will be upset to know you got into a fight again. Your forehead is swollen, too. Why can’t you take it easy with your friends, Abel?’ Jessy said in a sad tone. ”Even I feel sad when you get hurt.”

“Yea yea. Fine. Stop the drama now.” Abel ignored.

The four started back towards home. John and Shakun walked behind the siblings, who seemed to be so happy with each other. Shakun walked in silence behind them, completely swept away by their affection for each other.

"Abel is my best friend. He is everyone's favorite too." John spoke as though he had read her mind.

Shakun just smiled, unaware that her heart was still beating a new rhythm at a new pace.

8

The next morning, Shakun was in her nightdress when she answered the doorbell and saw John and Abel in all smiles. John waved to her, but her eyes could only see Abel standing in front of her. Once again, she felt the bubble burst and the new rhythm in her heart. Abel stood at the door, still smiling at Shakun. His million-dollar smile made her legs weak and she trembled.

"Good morning. Dream Girl," Abel said.

"Who is that, Shakun?" Appa asked from the living room.

"It's me, uncle. John."

"Aah,John. Come here, my boy. Want some coffee? I mean milk?"

"Milk? No uncle." John replied, feeling embarrassed.

"Who is this new boy with you?" Appa asked.

"I'm Abel, uncle. My house is just on the opposite side." Abel said in a respectful tone.

"Oh...ok. Which class are you both studying now?'"

"12th...John and I are in the same class."

"That's wonderful. Which school?"

"Little Hearts Higher Secondary"

"Oh! I have plans to visit your school tomorrow for Shakun's admission. However, I am concerned if there will be any chance for her as the admission date has passed." Appa said, pointing at Shakun.

"That's why we came to tell you that we can help you with that." Abel replied, sounding like a hero.

"How can you boys help me? I don't understand."

"Uncle.." John spoke in between.

"Abel's father is in America and donates a lot of money to school. He can speak to the principal for Shakun's admission."

"Really? That would be a wonderful favour, dear!" Appa smiled.

"I will tell dad to call and speak to our principal tonight. Our principal cannot say no to my dad." Abel said proudly.

"Oh! Have you got a telephone at home? That's nice." (telephones were a luxury those days)

"No, uncle. Dad calls at Naadaar uncle's bakery, every Friday night. I will tell him about her admission."

"That's excellent news. We will always be grateful to him for that. Please convey our thanks to your father when you speak to him tonight."

"Come. Have breakfast with us." Amma invited them with a welcoming smile.

"Aaah..Savitri! Did you hear what they said about school admission?" Appa asked excitedly.

"Yes, yes..I heard it all. Thank you, dears." Amma said gratefully to the boys.

The following week, Shakun joined 'Little Hearts', the best and nearest school, with her best and closest friends always around. For the new kid in town, life took a new turn.

From that point on, Jessy and Shakun became inseparable. Shakun's heart began to yearn to become inseparable from Abel, too. FOREVER.

9

Present day

Shakun woke up smiling and excited about her new determination to win Abel's heart. Winny had made her decide that, from now on, she would be the commander of her life. She felt like a soldier, ready to fight for her dreams. She will not give up on Abel like John gave up on Kavya. She will get her Abel back. Shakun never felt so sure of herself. She quickly got ready for school. Quick bath, quick look at her new self in the mirror, quick breakfast, quick peck on Amma's cheek, and quickly ran down to John's house. She could not wait to tell him about her God-sent dream and her decision to win Abel back.

Shakun peeked at John's mom through their kitchen window and asked politely. "Aunty….John?"

"He is not going to school today, Shakun. He has a fever. Still sleeping. Go and see."

"Oh….ok."

John's room was at the leftmost corner of their living room. Shakun walked towards his door and slowly opened it. John was sleeping on his left side, with his whole body covered under his blanket and curved into a C.

Shakun looked around his room and found it as shabby as it always was. Dirty clothes were pushed to one corner of his bed. His study table was littered with half-opened books and pencil dust. There was a glass of water, half filled, and another glass with turmeric milk, half empty. For his fever, supposedly. The only place that looked neat was his own tiny shoe rack, kept carefully next to his study table. She smiled and remembered how crazy John was about his shoes. The rack had 6 pairs of shoes of various brands and shades. All arranged in order of purchase. She imagined John naked, with only shoes on his legs. It made her giggle, but she quickly cupped her mouth and sat at the edge of his bed. His sleeping posture made him look like a giant snake rolled inside a basket.

"Aww…poor FAB… got a fever, eh? Or, did you see Kavya kissing Abel again? Did the hot couple make you HOT!!" She bent down, whispered into his hidden ears, and tickled him, knowing he was awake.

"Get lost! I'm already burning. Don't bother me." John spoke irritably from beneath the sheet.

"Oh, come on, FAB! I came to tell you something important. But now I have to wait till you get better." Shakun sighed, pushing his shoulders.

"Go tell Jessy. She is your bestie." John continued from under the sheet.

"Of course. She is amazing. However, I have things that I cannot tell her. I did not tell her about my love for Abel. Did I?"

John sat up, pulling his blanket down to his lap. His eyes looked swollen, and his hair was overgrown and clumsy all over his head.

Shakun touched his forehead with the backside of her palm.

'My God! You are really burning."

"That's called fever. Now, can you go? I want to sleep." With fallen shoulders, John pleaded.

"Fine. Sorry. I just wanted to let you know that I have decided to fight for Abel. That's all. Bye." Shakun stood up.

"Wait...what?" he asked, pulling her back to sit.

"What fight? Like dishum-dishum with Kavya? What are you saying, sis?" John laughed.

"Don't be stupid. Not that kind of fight. I am going to just focus on getting his attention first and then his..... " Shakun stopped and stared at John with her round eyes.

"Loooovee....." John whispered, shaping his fingers into a heart.

"Yes. That's right. But I really don't know how."

"I know what you can do. Just forget him and move on. That's the best for you."

"Wow..thanks, my dear bestie. Easy idea. But sorry, I'm not taking that. I am no longer a little girl who always follows your advice."

"Oh yes. I forgot. You are a big woman who knows everything about love and life."

Shakun just stared at John, whom she thought was the only person who understood her. She felt angry at his mockery, and her anger filled her eyes once again.

"I thought you would be excited for me and help me, Fab. Now I know you won't. You've never accepted my feelings for Abel.

But I do. I believe in myself and how I feel about him. I believe that I love him. Even God knows that I do. That's why He sent this dream and showed me a world without Abel in it. I felt the pain, Fab.. and it was so hurting. It felt like someone was choking me, and I could not breathe. I cannot imagine a life without Abel, Fab. I cannot…!!!!" Shakun spoke breathlessly.

"Hey, hey, stop stop! I am sorry. I was just trying to be funny. Please. Mummy might walk in anytime." John pleaded guilty.

"I know what you feel, sis, and I will help you. I promise," he assured her.

Shakun took a few seconds more to calm herself and looked at John with red eyes. She sniffed a little and smiled.

"You are the only one who knows everything about me..fab! So please don't ever speak to me like that again. I cannot forget Abel. Ok? I know I can be wrong, and maybe it is not love at all. But I care for him, and I feel sad to see him with someone else." Shakun spoke continuously.

"Okay okay… I got it. Let's go to school now. It's late already."

Oh, but you have a fever, don't you?'

"Fever? Who.. me?" John touched his own forehead.

"Looks like your tears washed my fever away," he joked with a wink.

"Ha ha..very funny. You rest and get well soon. I will see you later."

"Ok. But if you are really serious about winning him back, then you should start by just telling him that." John suddenly snapped.

"What?" Shakun stared into John's clear eyes.

"Yes.. Just tell him that you love him," he repeated, shrugging his shoulders.

Shakun had heard the same thing from Winny. She now felt compelled to take action.

John sounded very serious this time, and Shakun felt a shiver at the thought of facing Abel and confessing her most deep-rooted secret directly to him, which she had taken so long to share with her bestie, John himself.

Shakun hugged her bag tightly to her chest and got up to walk out of the room as though his words had struck lightning, paralysing her brain from reacting.

"Before all that, remember that you have your exam today. You better focus on that now. ok?" But Shakun walked away quietly past the same kitchen window without waving to his mom. She stepped out of the building and felt lost in the words that John had just said. Though she had felt determined the previous night, it never occurred to her that it would be as scary as it felt now.

10

She looked at her watch. It was getting late for school. She thought of Jessy and realised that she was at her cousin's house and would be dropped directly from there. Just as she wondered if she should walk to school or wait for a rickshaw, she saw Abel step out of his home. Once more, she heard the familiar whistle and the sound of keys twirling in his fingers. His face looked more handsome with each passing day.

"Why would Kavya give away this treasure... never. Damn! She is so lucky." Shakun frowned at her own misfortune.

Abel saw her standing alone and asked,

"Hi Shakun. Why are you standing alone with that angry face?" He smiled with wonder.

Shakun had once again made herself look silly.

"Nothing. I got late. Now looking for a rickshaw," she lied.

"Where is John?"

"He has a fever."

"Oh! But you won't get a rickshaw now. You can come with me. Jessy went to my aunt's place yesterday. So her seat is empty." Abel smiled, pointing to his bike's pillion.

Shakun could not believe what she just heard. Her dream was coming true once again. She felt a cool breeze blow over her. Suddenly, there was music in the air. So filmy and unreal! Her heart paced faster and her tummy tickled. She looked confused. Was God giving her this chance to tell him about her feelings? The thought made her shiver, and she stood perplexed. Something told her to just let go and tell him. She took a deep breath to get stronger.

"Hello....Dream Girl." Abel came close and snapped his fingers.

"Yea..yea... I can. Thank you." Shakun managed to get her words out.

"Come! Let's hurry, or you will be late for your exam."

Shakun did not care about her exam. She was living the moment with full awareness. She was in bliss. She gently lifted herself to sit back, struggling not to lose her balance.

"Your hands won't burn me, Shakun. You can hold on to my shoulders!" Abel said.

Shakun noticed that Abel had watched her through the mirror and saw her hesitate to place her hands.

She felt caught red-handed, and she slowly held on to his shoulders. Again the tummy ache, again the new heartbeat. She hid her face behind him, away from the front mirror, and smiled to herself. She was riding with her prince in his golden chariot, and he was carrying her away to his palace in the skies.

"I haven't seen you for so many days, and you didn't come home to see Jessy either. What happened?" Abel shouted through his helmet as he rode on.

She couldn't hear him because of the wind.

"What?"

"I was just asking if everything is fine with you."

"Yes. Why do you ask?" She shouted back.

"I have not seen you for a long time."

Shakun remained silent, unsure of how to express her ongoing anger towards him for the button incident.

"Will we be late?" Shakun changed the topic.

"My bike is faster than flight," he teased with pride. Shakun looked at him through the mirror and caught him looking back at her. The moments felt magical.

They finally reached school, and Shakun felt sad that her ride was over too soon. She got down without taking her hands away from his shoulders. She did not wish to let go of it. No, not so soon. But she had to.

Abel smiled a goodbye.

"Thank you, Abel." She said in a low voice

"Okay…"

Shakun started walking further, and she noticed Abel gazing at her. She turned and asked

"What...? Not going to class?"

"Actually, I wanted to say something."

Shakun felt a shiver run through her navel. She quickly looked down at her shirt. It was perfectly buttoned this time. Abel noticed her reaction and laughed.

"No, no, dear! In fact, I want to say sorry for that." He said, pointing to her shirt.

"I am sorry for that comment the other day. I know I embarrassed you. I didn't mean to."

Shakun did not want to relive that moment. She kept quiet, not knowing how to respond.

"Oh, wait a second... was THAT the reason you stayed indoors all these days?" Abel gaped with his mouth open.

Shakun quickly turned and started walking away when she heard him shout behind her.

"I am so sorry again, Shakun. But I should say you are growing into a gorgeous woman, Dream Girl! This time, I mean it. Bye."

Shakun kept walking, smiling at herself. She could not believe what she heard. After a long time, the same hope of being loved by her Prince Charming churned her insides again.'Oh my dear god! Did he just say that I look pretty?' Shakun felt like the world's most beautiful woman, frozen with pride and wishing to stay frozen forever.

She ran into the huge pillars of the open assembly hall without letting Abel see the tears of joy that had layered her beautiful big eyes. She realised that she had completely forgotten about her confession plan. After all, how could she remember anything else when she was flying high with him in the clouds.

She hid herself behind a pillar and slowly peeked out to see him pass by from the school bike parking area. She spotted him hurrying in the opposite direction towards the school's most popular mango tree. She saw Kavya standing with her friends. Shakun's heaven came crashing down once again. Abel joined Kavya, and they walked back to their assembly hall together. She observed how happy Abel was with Kavya. Confused, she turned and clashed on Jessy, who had been observing her the entire time. Jessy looked angry, and Shakun feared whether she understood what was going on.

“Hi, Jessy. I was looking for you.” Shakun muttered nervously.

“Of course... I saw you searching for me...haha!”' Jessy laughed and hugged Shakun, who sighed with relief.

Jessy is so dumb, she thought to herself. Thank God!

“Where's John? I haven't seen him either.”

“At home. Fever.”

“Oh, I had something interesting to tell him," she said, shrugging her shoulders and winking in the same way she usually does when she has gossip news to share.

“Offo...Jessy...let's go. By the way, how was your stay with your aunt? Did you study or did you just enjoy yourself?” Shakun distracted and dragged her away to class.

“Study? Never. Aunty took me to the movie yesterday. And I did not like it at all. Such a boring one.” Jessy bragged about her movie as they disappeared into their class.

11

The semester exams started without any study holidays in between. Shakun took it as a reason to postpone her confession to Abel. For the moment, she had something tougher in hand to deal with. Physics exam. Shakun found physics the most difficult subject of all. She never understood why she feared it so much. On the morning of her physics exam, Shakun, as usual, walked into the kitchen to pick up the coffee that Amma had made. She kissed her mom and took the coffee cup. As she turned to go back to her room, Amma noticed blood stains all over her nightgown.

"Shakun, wait. Come here." Amma took a second glance and said it joyfully.

"At last, you got your first period, my dear." Amma hugged her with tears of joy. She had begun to think of taking Shakun to a doctor for her slow growth. Shakun felt embarrassed by her mom's excitement as she shared with her all the dos and don'ts of menstrual cycles and the use of Carefree, which she had already learnt from her physically mature friend Jessy.

"Are you experiencing any stomach pain or cramps, dear?" I believe you should remain at home today.

Shakun had no pain or cramps, as told by Amma, but her naughty mind told her that it was the best chance to skip her exam, which she was afraid to attend.

"Yes, Amma. I'm feeling a little ill. But what about my exam? Appa won't agree." Shakun pretended to care.

Amma walked to Appa's side and whispered something into his ears. He glanced at Shakun and flashed a strange smile.

"It's better that you stay home with your mother today, dear. This is not your final exam anyway," Appa said, tapping her cheek. She smiled and escaped into her room, thanking her first period for its perfect timing.

It was mid-afternoon when Amma barged into Shakun's room and found her lying on her stomach reading her favourite comic, 'The Archies.'

"How is your stomach pain now, dear?"

Shakun closed her book with a bang and sat up facing her mother. It took her more than a moment to connect with what her mother was discussing.

"Oh, my stomach. Yes, the pain. It's... it's better now, Amma. Yea..much better"

"Why are you stammering like this?"

"Nothing. I was so deep into my book that you just scared me a little. Maybe you should knock the door next time."

"Aahaa…? I should knock on your door. Does that mean you have secrets to hide? Eh?"

"Oho..it's just basic manners, amma.."

"hmmm… Now that you have grown to be a woman, you are teaching me manners. Not bad," Amma mocked.

"Stop it, Amma. Don't make my periods a big deal. Ok?"

"It IS a big deal, Shakun. From now on, expect that we will limit your access to certain activities that you previously enjoyed."

"What do you mean?"

"I believe you should now exercise some control over your daily activities. Cut down on walking around with boys in the neighborhood. Likewise, boys coming home will not be allowed anymore. No sleeveless tops. No short skirts. You can only attend extra classes if Jessy is also with you. No group studies. No friends meet after 6 p.m. Most importantly, you cannot spend long hours of time at John's house, even though we are both well aware of the affection you share as siblings. So, these are the things I wanted to tell you."

Shakun could not stop staring at her new mom. She had never before heard her mother sound like a dictator. She rolled her eyes at her mom and shrieked.

"Amma, what is wrong with you? Just because I got my period does not mean I should change my relationship with people. Seriously, you have gone mad. That much I can see."

"Shakun, dear!" It was Appa's voice.

Shakun stood up instantly with respect. She was shocked to see her father walk into her room for the first time.

"Appa. What is Amma saying? New rules? New conditions? You please tell her to stop being so ridiculous."

"Okay, ok. Calm down."

Appa came closer to Shakun, holding her by the shoulders.

"Sit."

Shakun sat on the bed next to her dad, who was now smiling at her.

“Your mom and I come from a generation where women don't even glance at men. I have already shared with you the story of our marriage. Remember? But have we ever stopped you from talking to your male friends?” Shakun looked down, shaking her head, while Appa continued.

“We have always trusted you with the freedom we have given you. You can still talk to them and be friends with them. But do not encourage any kind of special attention from them. I am sure you understand what I am talking about. Everything is fine if you promise to always be on guard and not let the boys take you for granted.”

“Yes, yes, Appa. I understand. I promise not to get into trouble in any way.”

“Savitri, are you happy?” Appa turned back and winked at Amma, who smiled shyly.

“You always have your way with your daughter. As usual, you won and I lost.” Amma confessed.

“No, no, my dear wife. We all won as a family. Right, Shakun?”

“Yes Appa. I love you both.” Shakun hugged her parents tight, ignoring her inner voice that told her how good an actor she was.

12

The next morning, Shakun found John waiting for her at the gate. Though she knew that the news of her blossoming had reached every house, she was glad that FAB had not changed this daily routine.

“Good morning, Shakun. Feeling better?”John was so straight-forward with his concern that Shakun felt relieved of her inhibitions to face him.

“Yes. And you? Fever?”

“Aah, that was nothing. But mom wanted me to rest. Let’s go.”

As they walked to school, Shakun was just starting to get excited about sharing her bike ride experience with Abel when she noticed him being unusually quiet and lost in his thoughts.

“What happened, FAB? You look disturbed. Are you worried about missing classes and needing to catch up on notes?”

“Ha ha..that would be the last thing I would worry about.”

“Then what are you thinking?”

John sighed “Yesterday Abel came home to see me. He told me something that made me sad for him.”

Shakun stopped walking abruptly.

“What happened to Abel, FAB? Is everything okay?”

“Hey, yes, of course. Keep walking. In fact, what he told me might make you feel a little happier,” he said with a wink and smiled.

“Are you going to explain or confuse me?’ Shakun asked seriously.

“Okay, ok… “

John sighed and continued,

“Abel and Kavya had a fight yesterday. He saw her flirting with some other boy in class just before assembly time.”

Shakun could feel the excitement slowly build up inside her. But she controlled it.

“And?” She asked softly.

“You know Abel’s temper, right? He slapped her.”

Shakun stopped walking once again. Her feet trembled.

“What? Abel slapped Kavya? You mean a REAL slap?” Shakun could not believe her ears.

“That's exactly how I reacted too. But yes. He actually slapped her…. in front of the entire class.”

“And?” Shakun could not wait for the details.

“It seems Kavya got wild. She yelled that she did not like to be controlled by him. She blamed Abel for being possessive and announced her breakup with him in front of everyone in class. Abel was upset but did not expect this from her. I also find it hard to believe that Kavya could end their relationship so quickly. Just like that,” John snapped his fingers.

“Then what happened?”

“Then what? Abel also held on to his ego. He shouted back and thanked her for breaking up with him.” John shrugged his shoulders. “He is still in shock. It all ended too fast. Poor fellow”

“What's he going to do now?” Shakun asked curiously.

“I don't know. He just told me that he regrets slapping her, but he will not apologise or try to get back. He wants to be quiet and free for some time. I am just hoping that he doesn't lose his focus on his studies. Our board exams are not far away.”

John turned to Shakun, expecting her to look worried and sorry for Abel. Instead, he saw Shakun smiling. Her face glowed with a joy that had crossed all boundaries. She stood in bliss. She looked at the sky. Her white, wet cotton clouds had returned. And so was her prince on his horse. This time she saw his handsome face. That was Abel and he was smiling at her. He reached out his palm and called her.

Shakun smiled and stretched her hands towards the sky.

John continued to stare at her and burst out laughing. His loud laughter shook Shakun from her trance. She saw her hands pointing to the sky and felt embarrassed.

John was still laughing uncontrollably.

“Oh my God!” John slowly calmed down and said

“What in heaven was that, Dream Girl? You looked like ‘The Statue of Liberty.' John imitated her posture with his hands raised and laughed once more. “You are so funny.”

“But you know what?” John said in a serious tone. “You are so mean to be happy about what happened between them. You are cruel and selfish, Shakun. Though I loved Kavya, I feel sad for Abel. I feel sorry for him that Kavya did not value his love."

"Yes John." Shakun stiffened. She walked close to John, looked into his eyes, and firmly whispered. "You are right. I am mean and selfish. That's because I know that my love for Abel is deep and sincere, unlike Kavya's. And even God knows that no one else can love him as much as I do. Kavya HAD to go, John. It's God's plan. Can't you see? Abel deserves the best. And that's ME!!! I have willingly prayed for this breakup to happen, and God has heard me now." Shakun rolled her eyes, which were beginning to fill with tears.

John stood stunned. Shakun called him 'John' only when she spoke about serious things. He looked back into her eyes and saw the despair in them.

"Ok ok… I am sorry. Calm down. I thought you were strong enough to confess your love directly to Abel. What happened to that?"

"I have not built enough courage for it yet, FAB."

"Hmmm... I know it's not easy."

After a brief pause, John said excitedly. "I will tell him.'

"What?" Shakun trembled.

"Yes. I will tell him about your feelings. And he knows very well how close we are. So he will take it seriously. That's for sure." John's face brightened with pride at finding the perfect solution to Shakun's confusion.

"No!! No, I'm not sure, Fab." Shakun felt her bile rise up to her throat. She shivered at the thought of Abel knowing about her long, secret love for him. “Is this the right time to tell him such a thing? And you just told me that he prefers to be free and left alone now. What if he gets annoyed with me? What if he starts to avoid me or stop talking to me? I won't be able to bear that. No fab. Please don’t.”

John forcibly held her shoulders and turned her to face him.

“Look. Given our close relationship, it would be most natural for him to learn about it from me. And of course I won't tell him that you and I planned it this way. Simple.”

Shakun still stood confused.

“Trust me on this, sis. What are brothers for otherwise?” John sounded promising.

Shakun slowly nodded to say yes and smiled.

“But will you tell him today?”

“Don't be in such a hurry, sis. It's time to prepare for the board exam. I will not tell him anything that will disturb his concentration. Your love will capture his attention only after our exams are over. So be patient. Let's just go to school now.”

Both walked the rest of the distance quietly. They reached the school gate, and John waved a bye to Shakun and walked away towards their class. Shakun waited and watched John join Abel, who had been waiting at the bike parking slot. She saw them hug and get into their exam hall. ‘Don't be sad, Abel. I am here for you. Always,’ she mumbled to herself.

“Shakuuunnn...Shakuuunnn....’ Jessy ran towards her from behind and hugged her tight.

"What Jessy? Why are you screaming like this?"

Jessy's excitement seemed uncontrollable, and her glee once again reminded Shakun of her physical transition.

Shakun shut Jessy's mouth with her palm and pulled her aside. She wondered how everyone knew about it. It was embarrassing.

"I'm thrilled to see you back at school. Don't worry, Shakun. All the boys know it too." Jessy teased with a wink.

"Please Jessy. Can I just have a normal day?"

"Yea yea. However, today will be your day to shine." She laughed hysterically, and both walked into class together.

Shakun followed her silently, still thinking about what John had told her and what was in store for her future. Would Abel accept her, or would he just tap her cheeks and say, 'Grow up, my little Dream Girl!'

13

The school ambience was quiet and serious for the next couple of months. The preparation for 12th grade board exams had begun. There were no longer any cultural events, enjoyable evenings with friends, or casual group discussions. It was that time of the year when the most notorious kids took copies of lessons from friends to finish up their incomplete work. It was that time when most parents are taken aback by their young adults' sudden shift to a study schedule that leaves little time for fun or friends, and that time when all the kids give their teachers and parents hope for better scores. It was the only time of year when all high schoolers began to worry about their future.

As the exam days passed by, Shakun kept her fingers crossed and prayed for Abel. She did not wish to disturb John for the next few days. Every morning Shakun sat on Winny's lap and watched John ride pillion with Abel as they had to reach their exam centre earlier for their exams. She was sure John would not have told Abel anything yet, fearing it would affect Abel's preparations. Or, even if he did, would it matter to Abel? she wondered. Fingers crossed!

It was mid-April, the month of scorching heat, sweaty shirts, and muddy shoes. It was the last exam day of the academic year for the whole school. Some looked confident about passing off with excellent scores. Some were unconcerned about the results and were just pleased that it was over and done. Long hours of locked-up preparations and late-night revisions were over, and the day brought back all the lost cheer and laughter. Every student threw their books high in the air as part of the routine of bidding farewell to learning and to welcome the fun time of the summer holidays. There were high fives and hurrahs, smiles and shouts, laughter and excitement.

But for the 12th graders, it was the last day of their entire school life. The whole crowd came back to school from their respective exam centres and gathered under the school mango tree. Some shook hands, wishing each other luck; some hugged and cried out loud, not willing to accept that their lives will take different directions from now on. They exchanged future plans, passing on tiny, rectangular-bound books with golden pages called 'The Autograph book,' to friends to record their wisdom quotes. Some jotted down their address and phone number (only the wealthy possessed a phone connection), yearning to maintain the same closeness as they had during their school days. An absurd silence wafted through the air. It had never occurred to them that they would, one morning, wake up to a crossroad like when friends would unclutch their tightly held fists to leave each other on the even more treacherous edge of life. Time had committed its crime once again.

However, Abel seemed oblivious to all the emotional turmoil of his fellow friends. His eyes stayed on Kavya, who was engrossed in a warm hug with her bestie girlfriend. Abel still could not believe that Kavya had actually broken up with him. Was it not right of him to get furious with her when she flirted with somebody else? Was that not proof of his love for her? John noticed Abel lost in his own thoughts and purposefully coughed to attract his attention.

“Still?” John shrugged his shoulders at Abel.

“I don't know. She is driving me crazy.”

“No, she is not. It's just you who cannot let go of her.”

“Exactly.”

“Oh, come on. Some people are not meant for each other. Ok? Maybe it's all for your good, or maybe... maybe there is someone better waiting for you.”

“Eh? What?”

“Nothing. Can we go home? I mean, if you are done staring at her?” John pointed to Kavya.

“Wait! So that's how you could so easily let go of Kavya? You think somebody better is waiting for you?” Abel had for the first time acknowledged John’s love for Kavya.

“Yes. I believe that we always get what is best for us.” John reassured Abel.

“Hmm..maybe. I am feeling better already. But I really want to talk to her. For one last time. A final goodbye. Please John.”

“Ok! Go and finish it once for all. I will wait for you at the exit gate.”

“Great! Thanks, John.” Abel walked away winking.

“And remember not to slap her again.” John warned.

“Urrghh! I have saved that for you, buddy.” Abel shouted back.

Abel ran back and looked for Kavya, holding on to that tiny speck of hope that he would find her in their usual special corner of privacy, waiting for him. He felt like a young hero yearning for his love to return. It was the perfect scene of filmy romance when an unexplainable desperation suddenly fondles the hearts of both lovers. They forget their flaws, forgive their faults, and run towards each other at the same time in slow motion. He would then look into her eyes and see them fill with remorse before quickly embracing her back into his life. Abel smiled to himself. Yuck!

“Looking for Kavya?” somebody tapped Abel from behind.

“Hey, Hari! Yes. Any idea where she is?”

“I saw her heading towards our classroom... with Arun.”

Abel stared at Hari, running his palm across his forehead, confused by the tone in which he spoke.

“Aah ok! It's just to say goodbye. After all, you know, right?” Abel shrugged his shoulders to defend his embarrassment.

“Hmmm. I know. But it's better you don't go there now.”

Hari's warning triggered Abel once again. Something inside him was burning. The filmy slow motion run abruptly ended.

Abel ran towards their classroom, hoping not to see anything that his mind was showing him and fearing that he would. He sprinted through the huge pillars of the assembly hall and took a short cut to the 4th floor, avoiding the eyes of many teachers and friends scattered all over the place.

When he reached the long corridor preceding his classroom, he realised the sudden quietness around him. All the classroom doors were closed. Abel saw that the door of his classroom was slightly ajar. The white painting of 12A on the door pinched his heart. A whole year of joyful days, sad stories, nasty fights, and group hugs suddenly felt overwhelming. But the fear of what might be happening inside at that moment pinched him back to the present. He raised his hand to open the door wider, and he heard their whispering voices.

"I love you and will miss all the wonderful times we had, Kavya."

"Hmm. I love you, Arun. I am going to miss you too."

"Really? I am flattered. Thank you. But are you sure you don't love Abel anymore?"

"I LIKED him, Arun! Not LOVED. It's not my fault that he got me all wrong."

"Wrong? The whole school was aware that you two were deeply in love and extremely possessive of each other."

"No. Not me. I hated him controlling me. I cannot love anybody who does not let me live my life in my own way." Kavya sighed and continued.

"Anyway, I am pleased that school is over. I never have to see him again. Thank God!"

Abel turned and walked away quietly letting the words fade into the distance and completely drowning into the pain it caused. Tears rolled down his cheeks as Kavya's words echoed much louder through the distance. 'She never loved me? Really? No..that can't be true'. He lost control of his mind and heart, as her words hit him hard again and again. Abel could no longer handle this hurtful truth of being duped by the only person whom he had always been honest with. He ran down the stairs, wishing he could just disappear into thin air. If this was the essence of love, he no longer desired it. It was over and done!

Abel panted as he rushed out of the exit gate and hugged John tight from behind. He did not want John to see him cry this way. John pulled him forward to face him, and he saw his bestie sobbing with his head bent down. John immediately knew what had happened. He forced Abel to look up and held his cheeks in his palms.

“Abel! She never deserved you. Let her go.” John insisted.

Abel hid his head on John's chest and slowed down his gasps for breath.

“Come on, let's get out of here before anyone sees you cry like a baby.”

14

It had been a week since school closed for vacation, and many had packed off to their respective native villages and towns to get bored with their grandparents, while the parents stayed back to enjoy their long-lost privacy of romantic late nights. The scorching Madras heat seeped its prickly rays through every sweaty scalp, and the city prayed that the summer would scroll its days faster. People were always worn out and thirsty. Many rushed their children to hospitals for dehydration treatments. It was always that time of year when children had the entire day to play, but instead, they chose to stay indoors, feeling bored. The streets were quiet during the day, with hardly a vegetable vendor pushing his cart of sad and burnt-out vegetables to some tiny shade under a tired tree.

Shakun sat on Winny's lap and looked down towards Abel's house. The huge mango tree on their open lawn had started to bear bunches of tiny raw mangoes. The tree covered half of the view into Abel's house, but she could still see a little bit of their kitchen door and the feet of the person who walked across their living room. She could see the feet and identify who they belonged to. If she saw a foot half covered with a saree, it was Jessy's mom. If she saw a foot with anklets, it was Jessy herself, and the strong, long one with socks belonged to Abel. He always kept his feet covered with socks, which made Shakun wonder if he had a missing toe. And even if he does, she would love him the same.

It was post-lunch time now, and Shakun wondered where Abel was. She always knew when, where, and what John and Jessy did, but not Abel. Sometimes even John and Jessy wouldn't know where Abel was, and it never bothered either of them. Jessy just knew that he goes to some friend's house every morning and comes back late in the evening. Nothing more, nothing less. Shakun wished she could spend more time at Jessy's place so that she could see Abel when he came back home. And now she knew that both Jessy and John would be napping after their heavy, meaty lunch. So she sat alone, bored, staring at the quiet world outside with her cheeks pressing on to Winny, when she heard the honk of Abel's bike from afar. She could recognise it even amidst a thousand bikes that passed by. She was surprised, as it was unusual of Abel to come back home at this hour.

Abel parked his bike in front of his gate. Shakun watched him get off the bike and slowly walk towards his house, when he suddenly stopped and turned back to look up at her. In shock, Shakun slid off Winny's lap and stood up, frozen in his gaze. She did not have time to wonder how Abel realised that she was sitting up there. With her heart pounding a thousand beats, she stood stunned as he kept looking up at her. A gush of hot afternoon air blew his hair all over his marble brown eyes, and he quickly brushed it away before it made him look silly. Shakun could feel more butterflies in her stomach as she got anxious about his next move. He quickly waved at her, leaving her feeling locked into his gaze. Shakun waved back, watching him slowly detach his gaze. He looked down and smiled shyly to himself as he walked into his home. She saw that he had tried to hide his smile. But why? Something felt different. Shakun wondered what he meant by that smile. Did he mean to say, 'What a silly girl she is to get all the wrong ideas,' or 'How did I miss noticing her all these days?' She stood there lost in her confusion, wondering if she was alive or dead in this filmy moment of magic. She held Winny with both hands and kissed her iron bars. 'Something has changed for sure, Winny! Did you see him smile at me? I think Fab has told him about my feelings for him. Yes. He knows. Yes, yes... at last!!'

Shakun jumped down the stairs and ran to John's house. It was quiet. After lunch, everyone was napping. She tiptoed to John's room and found him sleeping with drools of saliva dripping from the corner of his mouth. "Uurrggh.' She felt nauseous. She closed her eyes with one hand and touched his shoulders with the other.

"Fab…Fab…." she whispered. No response.

"John…" she blew into his ears.

"Eh..eh..what..what..?" John yelled and sat up in panic, eyes wide open.

"It's me... it's me. Shakun."

"Jesus!… You scared me, idiot!"

Shakun rolled her eyes, realising he had never used such harsh words on her before.

"Sorry." John apologised as he wiped away his drool and smoothed out his dishevelled hair.

"What happened now?" John looked at her with concern.

Shakun just smiled shyly at him, thinking that he would understand the meaning of her smile and would admit talking to Abel about her.

"Ey…what? Why are you smiling like this? Paithiyama?" (Are you mad?)

"I know what you did. So don't pretend. Ok?"

"What? What did I do?"

"Come on, fab! I know you told Abel."

"What did I tell Abel?"

"Stop it, fab! Don't irritate me. The way he looked at me today, I know that you have told him."

"You are the one irritating me. You simply barge in whenever you feel like it and then wake me up to engage in puzzles. I haven't told Abel anything about you yet, okay? I swear. Because I have to stay home and help dad, I haven't seen him much. You know that. And he is always out somewhere; no one knows where." John bombed, pointing his fingers towards her face.

Shakun stared into his eyes and started to wimp. It was the first time that John had shouted at her.

"Why did he give me that shy smile today, Fab? Why did he look at me like he had never before? Was all that once again just my imagination?" Shakun broke down.

"I am sure it is. And it's better that he does not know about you now."

"What? Why?"

"Didn't Jessy tell you? I thought she would have."

"Don't scare me, Fab. Does Abel have a new girlfriend?"

"No...no..that's not it." John smiled.

"Then? What is it?"

"He is leaving India to settle in America very soon. With his dad. He is trying to join some college there."

"What? What are you saying, John? That cannot be true at all. Even Jessy did not tell me anything till now. So it can't be true. Someone has just made a joke about it to you." Shakun continued breathlessly denying any possibility of her prince leaving her for ever.

"Come to your senses, Shakun. Maybe Jessy did not tell you because she and aunty do not wish to go now. Only Abel is."

"But he smiled at me differently today. He seemed to be growing fond of me." Shakun stood firm, not letting her magic moment turn into a dream once again.

"Sshhhh...stop it." John held her shoulders and whispered to calm her.

"Who told you this? I want to know. Please" Shakun pleaded.

"Abel himself told me on the last day of school. He said he is heartbroken and he hates to be here now. It seems his dad also feels there are better colleges for him there"

"Oh, so it's true. What was the meaning behind that smile, Fab?" Shakun paused and let her tears drop on the floor.

"Maybe he has just realised that he will miss you as much as he will miss us. That's all. Now that you know the truth, does it make any difference?" John sighed and got out of bed.

"If that's true, then I definitely want you to tell him. I want him to know that I love him dearly. I don't care about how he feels or what he says. I just want him to know. That's all," Shakun shrieked, losing control of her emotions.

"Okay, okay. Don't shout. Mom will wake up." John covered her mouth and smiled wide.

"Shall I go now and tell him right away?" He joked to make her smile.

"I saw him go home. You can. I am not afraid anymore." Her words were calm and firm.

"Hmmm…not bad. Then tell him yourself."

"No no… I tried, and I realised I cannot." Shakun confessed and laughed.

"I'll talk to him at church tomorrow. Okay? Happy? Go home now. I don't want to share my snacks with you." John gave his order, walked out, and waved for her to follow. Shakun yelled in joy and rushed back home. She sat on Winny's lap and whispered, 'Fab will talk to Abel tomorrow. I feel so scared, Winny. Will he love me?' She hugged Winny tight and felt the warmth of love all around her.

15

It was the same slow Sunday morning when John stretched himself out of his blanket and smiled at the small clock on his table that pushed its needles to 8. a.m. That was a long sleep. He wore his shirt, pulled up his shorts, and walked out with a toothbrush in his mouth. There was a tap beside their gate for all visitors to wash their feet before they entered his house. John spat the foamy paste out of his mouth and splashed water on his face to freshen up. He walked to the gate and pulled out the newspaper that was tucked in.

"Good morning, John," he heard Jessy shout from across the street.

"Same to you," he smiled. "You look pretty in that dress."

"Abel said I look fat," she said, laughing.

John clicked his tongue to say no. "Why are you standing out?"

"We are off to church. I got ready early. Are you not coming?" Jessy asked loudly.

"Why are you screaming like this? Yes, I will, but later." John replied softly.

"Don't be too late. Abel comes only because you are there too." Jessy reminded.

"Ha ha..I know," John laughed.

As she spoke, Jessy looked up to the first floor of John's house, and she saw Shakun standing at the window, waving at her. Jessy waved back with a broad smile.

"I'm going to church. Will come over after lunch." She shouted, looking upward.

"Ok. I like your dress. You look beautiful." Shakun yelled back, throwing a flying kiss towards her.

Shakun saw Abel from her window, holding his mom's hand and walking towards their gate. Aunty looked gorgeous. Draped in a dark green sari, she camouflaged with the green leaves as they walked under their mango tree. Shakun got her eyes glued to Abel. She wondered why she found him more and more handsome each day. Abel wore a sky blue full-sleeve shirt neatly tucked into his black Raymond pants. With his sleeves folded to his elbow, his arms looked muscular. As they reached their gate, the morning summer breeze spoiled his neatly combed silky hair. He brushed it upwards with his hands, and that's when he saw Shakun at her window. He caught her staring at him and smiled. Shakun suddenly felt John, Jessy, and Aunty disappear in a flash. It was only she and Abel now. Their eyes glued to each other, trying to read each other's minds. Abel threw a flying kiss, and Shakun covered her face with blushing hands.

Abel clapped and called out for a rickshaw, breaking Shakun's trance once again. She felt foolish for harbouring such fantasies. She tapped her head slightly and looked down at the real world. Jessy and her mother got into the rickshaw, while Abel whispered something to John, and they burst out laughing. Shakun loved his laughter and felt she could drown in the whirlpool of his deep dimples. Jessy peered out of the three-tyred vehicle and looked up to wave a bye to Shakun, while Abel pushed her further in to get more space for himself.

'Don't be late to church, John.' Abel reminded John, and the rickshaw pulled away from them.

As Shakun watched Abel go, she felt her heart leave her body and follow him. 'What is this love all about that is making me feel so lonely when he leaves? Why do I want him near me all the time? Why?' Shakun ran inside and fell on her bed. She hugged her pillow tight and closed her eyes. She could feel her heart thumping against the cushion. She replaced the pillow with Abel, and her excitement grew. She hugged Abel so hard and kissed his chest, which felt tight and strong under her lips. She looked at him tenderly as he smiled and pulled her up to his face. She stared into his brown marble eyes, which were just inches away from hers. She saw love brimming in them. She saw that they were asking her for something. Something new. Something she had never given to anyone till now. Something that she did not know how to give. Abel looked down at her lips. With his hand behind her head, he drew her close. He gently placed his lips on hers, and her world began to spin.

"AMMUUUU..." her mother called out from the kitchen, and she sat up on her bed with a jerk. She looked down at her pillow, which was now crumpled and shapeless. She felt it look back with a frown, and she giggled. She gently rubbed her hands on the pillow and whispered, 'Did I hurt you, dear? I am sorry.' She cupped her mouth and laughed.

"Shakun…." her mother called her again.

"Coming maa… I can hear you."

It was post-lunch time. Shakun became restless and wondered why John had not come to meet her. She imagined the worst of things that Abel could have told him after hearing about her feelings for him from John. She wanted to run down and talk to John, but the thought of hearing something negative from him scared her. She was lying on her bed with her stomach facing down, engrossed in her favourite Archies comic, when Jessy, as promised, barged into her room and jumped on top of her with excitement. She looked over Shakun's shoulder and peeked into the page she had been reading. It was the most perfect one, with a picture of Archie and Ronnie in a tight liplock with 'Smack' written on top.

“Whattaakiss..eh?” She screamed into Shakun's ears.

Shakun rolled her eyes and closed the book with a thud. She struggled to push Jessy away from her back, but she was unable to do so.

“Oh God! You are so heavy, Jessy! Get off my back.”

“Ha ha... I am not heavy, my dear. You are weak.” Jessy teased back into her ears.

“Fine..now get off... urrrggghhhh..please.” Shakun tried to roll both sides to push her away.

“Okay..okay. I just can't have fun with you.” Jessy let her go, and she sat on the bed.

“How was your Sunday mass?” Shakun changed the topic and got out of bed.

“As usual. But I came running because I had something to tell you.” Jessy looked at her and slowly widened her eyes.

“Ohh…no no no no….” Shakun folded her hands to say she was not interested.

“No Shakun. This time it’s not just gossip. I am really concerned.” Jessy spoke in a serious tone.

Shakun had never heard Jessy talk in such a tone. She gazed directly into Jessy's eyes and enquired

“What is it, Jessy? You look worried.”

“It’s Abel.”

Shakun's heart began to race. John has done it. He has told Abel about her. Shakun pretended to be patient.

“What about him? Did he tell you anything?” She enquired suspiciously.

“That’s the problem. He has been silent since we returned from church.”

“Why? What happened there?” Shakun knew something terrible had happened, and it was because of her.

“ I don't know. But it all started after John spoke to him. John reached church when mass was almost over. We left after Amen, and mom started talking to the other aunties. John joined us, and after a few seconds, he quickly dragged Abel to the far corner of the church wall.” Jessy explained, and Shakun’s heart began to palpate again. “John was saying something very seriously, and Abel looked shocked. They were arguing about something, I am sure.” Jessy narrated. Shakun shivered with the thought. ‘He did it. FAB told him for sure. Oh God!’

"Why? What did John tell him?" She spoke pretentiously.

"I couldn't hear anything from that distance. But since then, Abel looks so lost and confused. I asked him so many times, but he said nothing."

"It may be some boy stuff that he cannot tell you." Shakun joked to lighten the moment.

"Seriously? You think boy stuff would quieten my brother like this? The Great Hero, Abel? No way. It's definitely a girl matter."

"I am sure he will tell you after some time." Shakun calmed her down.

"I don't know. He has just locked himself up in his room since the time we came from church." Jessy said, knuckling her fingers, when a sudden thought struck her mind, and she said,

"Shakun, you are close to John than me. Can you ask him for me?"

""What? Why should I ask him?" Shakun stressed on the 'I'

"Ok, fine. I will ask him. You come with me. Let's go now."

"Now? Why? Just calm down, Jessy."

"No. I can't relax until I understand the situation. I am going down now." Jessy said firmly.

"Wait Jessy. Don't be stubborn like this. Please." Shakun pleaded and pulled her back.

Jessy stared at Shakun. She felt something suspicious. She saw fear in Shakun's eyes, which spoke more than her words.

"Aaah! Now I understand. You actually know what John has told my brother. Correct? John already told you about it. I can see that in your eyes." Jessy turned around and clapped for herself. "Now I know that you know. And that you haven't told me all the while, even though I am your best friend." Jessy pointed at her angrily.

"Noooo… I don't know anything. I don't know what John has told your brother. I swear!" Shakun pinched her throat in despair.

"I am going down to ask John. Are you coming?" Jessy demanded.

Shakun shivered and prayed that John should not be home.

"Okay," she said helplessly.

Jessy ran down the stairs, skipping steps in between, and Shakun took her time, wishing some miracle happened to escape this situation.

John's mom opened the door, rubbing her eyes. The hot afternoons made everyone sleepy.

"Aunty, we want to meet John. Is he there?" Jessy startled her.

"If he is not with your brother, he should be here."

Jessy and Shakun smiled at her, then walked past her into John's room.

16

They stormed into his room, finding him lying on his bed with his legs crossed, his sleeveless baniyan exposing half of his chest hair, and his trousers revealing most of his fat thighs. He was reading the most popular Tamil magazine. Aanandha Vikadan. The book was rated highly for gossip, movie star news, and other short stories about love, adultery, and crime.

Jessy walked in angrily and snatched the book out of John's hands. He sat up straight, trying to understand what had just happened, and saw Jessy with her hands behind her back, hiding the book.

John's eyes widened to see both of them together in his room. Jessy hardly came into his room for anything. She would just call him from the main door or sit in the living room whenever she visited him. The sudden appearance of both girls in his room startled John, and he became conscious of his appearance. He grabbed his lungi, which was attached to a thin rope tied from the window bar on one corner to a nail hammered on the opposite sidewall, and wrapped it around him.

"Why can't you knock before you bang the door open, girls?" he shouted as he tied up his attire.

"We did not think that you would be half naked like this." Jessy snapped and giggled. They quickly turned their backs to him.

John pulled a shirt from his cupboard and wore it.

"Ok. Now tell me what happened—that you both have come here so urgently."

"Fab...she wants to..." Shakun wanted to hint at John not to tell her, but Jessy placed a hand on her mouth.

"You be quiet. I will do the talking. Ok?" Jessy interrupted and stared into Shakun's face. Shakun feared the worst. She froze.

"What's going on? Why are you both acting so strange today?" John asked.

"John, be honest with me. What did you tell my brother at church today?" Jessy asked firmly.

John did not expect such a direct question from her.

"What...what do you mean...when?" John looked at Shakun and stammered.

"This morning, after Mass, when my mom and I were talking to others, I saw you dragging Abel away. Why? And what did you tell him?" Jessy hit his shoulder.

Shakun tried to pull Jessy away from him. "Jessy please…!"

"Nothing. We were just talking like every other time." John said casually as he sat on his bed.

Jessy stood in front of him and looked close to his face.

"No, John. That is a lie. You are lying. I know that. Abel never hides anything from me. But today, you said something that has made him look so quiet. You have to tell me what that was?" Jessy got louder this time.

"I am NOT LYING. And I did not tell him anything that he couldn't share with you." John shouted back. He was frustrated this time. He did not like Jessy's demanding tone. He found

Jessy completely different from Shakun in all ways. Jessy was louder , cleverer and more courageous than Shakun. She can at one time be like the sweetest, chirpy little girl and instantly shift to being big, bitchy, and wild.

"Yes, you are! You are a LIAR!!" Jessy screamed into his face. Shakun panicked. She feared that Jessy could turn violent at any moment, causing things to spiral out of control. She was capable of that. Shakun closed her ears with her hands, looked down, and boldly let the golden words out of her mouth.

"I love Abel. And that's what Fab told him today at church."

That's it! It was stated and done. The burden she carried since the first time she saw Abel was suddenly dropped. She felt free. At last!! Now whatever may happen. She stood there quietly, with head down and eyes closed, scared to even look at Jessy. After a few seconds of silence, she opened her eyes to see Jessy in shock, staring at her face. Shakun had just taken a step towards Jessy when John's mother rushed in.

"Why are you three shouting like this? What happened?"

"Nothing mummy. It's just our normal stuff. You don't get worried," John hurried to her with a fake smile. Jessy followed and hugged her.

"Best friends always fight Aunty. It's normal," she said in a funny tone.

Aunty looked towards Shakun.

"And why are you looking sad, dear? Did your FAB fight with you? You tell me, and I will hit him, ok?" she said, hugging her. Shakun had always been her favourite hypothetically adopted daughter. She was always pleased and proud that John found a sibling connection with her.

“No, no, aunty. He can never fight with me.” Shakun glanced at John, who was still frowning at Jessy.

“Ok then. All of you come and have tea with us. Come.” Aunty pushed them out of the room and rushed back to the kitchen.

“No, it's ok, aunty. I am going home. Mummy and Abel will be waiting.” Jessy said it loudly, without smiling.

Shakun quickly held Jessy’s hand to stop her. She wanted to read her thoughts. Jessy stared at her, and thin tears began to form. She pulled herself free from Shakun’s grip and walked out of the room, not knowing if she should be angry with her for loving her brother or for keeping it a secret from her. Shakun could feel the pinch of guilt that her heart endured. She felt responsible for her best friend's sense of deceit and mistrust.

John felt totally confused about what had happened. He did not try to stop Jessy. They walked behind her until she quietly stepped out of the gate.

“Jessy ... I am sorry. Please!!” Shakun’s voice broke as she saw Jessy crossover and disappear into her home.

After he was sure that Jessy had gone, John bit his teeth and whispered hurriedly into Shakun’s ears.

“Why did you suddenly break in and tell her about Abel, Shakun? Can’t you not wait till I tell Abel myself?” John said angrily.

Shakun gazed at John with wide eyes, spellbound by his serious gaze. She felt a shock wave pass through her guts. She wondered if she heard him right.

“What? What do you mean? Did you not tell Abel about me?” Shakun rolled her eyes at John, and her heart began to palpate in its fastest rhythm.

“No. I did not,” he lifted his shoulders and said in a casual tone. Shakun felt her brain would burst any moment. She walked closer to John and spoke softly.

“No no no no… Don’t play with me now, John.”

John saw that Shakun was upset with him.

“I am not. I did not talk to Abel about you today at church. I swear.” John spoke as honestly as he could.

“Urrrrgghhh,” Shakun clutched her hair with both hands. She did not understand what had happened. She knew she had made a fool of herself and was going to be in great trouble. She looked up at John, who was staring at her.

“What's all this drama about, John? What did you actually tell him then?” She pleaded.

“Look sis!” It was John's turn to be serious. He held her by the shoulders in order to get her attention.

“I had met Kavya at the market yesterday evening, and she had told me that she wanted to meet Abel to tell him that she had made a mistake. That she wanted Abel to forgive her. She wanted me to talk to Abel for her because she was too ashamed to talk to him by herself. I felt sorry for her and told

Abel about it at church. It was nothing about you, Shakun. I am sorry."

Shakun stood aghast with what she heard. Everything seemed so wrong. She could not believe that Kavya was coming back to Abel's life. She couldn't believe it was happening now, when she had every opportunity to win him over.

"What should I do now, Fab? Jessy will definitely tell her brother, and he will hate me forever." Her tears could stop no more. Shakun covered her face and sobbed.

John looked towards his home. He didn't want his mother to come out and witness her tears.

"Don't cry, Shakun. Please. Whether I tell him or Jessy, it won't make a difference to him. In fact, it's better if he hears it from his favourite sister than me."

"But why would she speak to him in my favour when she herself is angry with me for it? It's over. All over. Forever." Shakun wiped her cheeks and walked back home silently. John stood there helplessly and watched her go.

17

Shakun climbed the stairs and sat on Winny's lap. She held onto Winny and placed her head on Winny's hexagon grills. A while ago, the hard metal felt warm, like Abel's kiss in her dream. She sat there and stared into Abel's home below. She had never felt as alone as she did since moving here. Suddenly there was no Abel, no Jessy, and no Fab. She felt a new sense of emptiness within herself. She let her guilt engulf her for hurting her dear Jessy. Guilt for blaming John for it. She felt remorse for not having the courage to discuss her feelings for Abel with him directly. It was all her own fault, and she did not have any right to throw it on anybody else.

Shakun searched for some movement in Abel's house through the green leaves of the huge mango tree. She felt that the tree was probably the only thing that seemed to be happy now, with all her new leaves and baby mangoes hanging in bundles. It seemed to sway joyfully, not just because of its fruiting time but also because of its life on Abel's lawn. Shakun felt it laughing at her for being such a fool in everyone's eyes. She thought it was shooting words at her. 'You are such a loser, Shakun! All you can do is sit on Winny's lap and stare into this house. What's stopping you from talking to Abel yourself? Why do you want the whole world to do it for you? Love is fearless. It is pure and powerful. It is the only emotion that creeps into human hearts without any warning. Love is not a mistake, and it is never anybody's fault. So let it go. Be bold. Just tell Abel that you have always loved him more than anybody else. If you believe in your love, Abel will be yours. The universe will make that happen.' Shakun looked deep into its swaying leaves and felt a gentle breeze blow on her face. She received a message that she already understood. She closed her tired eyes. It was not even a minute that she dozed when she heard the thumping sound of her dad climbing up the steps, coming back from somewhere she was unaware of.

"Why are you always sitting here, Ammu? Don't you feel hot? Come in."

Shakun looked at him with her puffy eyes, smiling blankly. Dad bent down and frowned with his eyebrows.

"Why is your eye red? Were you crying?"

"Crying? No, appa. I am just bored and sleepy," she pretended.

"Hmm…it's all magic of the heat." Dad patted her shoulder and took her inside.

Shakun was proud that she could easily fool her dad. Poor dad. If only he knew what kind of a brat his daughter was.

Amma was making her usual Sunday snack pakoras when Dad smelt the aroma of their flavours and walked into his room.

"Where were you all the while, Shakun? Down at John's?" she enquired, focussing on her frying pan. "You should not be spending too much time there. They might start to think you are a nuisance. What do you do there, anyway?"

"Jessy was also there, Amma. We were just talking." Shakun joined her mom in the kitchen.

"Then why did John's mom come up and tell me that you were fighting? Not just talking." Amma sounded serious this time.

Shakun looked at her with surprise.

“Oh. When did she come here?”

“Doesn't matter. Is it true?”

“Nothing, ma. Just small stuff. You know how possessive Jessy is. She was upset that I spent more time with John than her. That's all.’

“Hmmm..that’s exactly what I say too. You don't go to Jessy’s house, do you?”

‘“How can I when she is always here with me, eh?” Shakun giggled.

“That's true too.” Mom smiled.

“But, Shakun, sometimes it's not just about being with your friends when you visit. It's also to get friendly with the other people in the family. Jessy comes here and spends time with me and your dad. But you hardly meet her mom. Even that’s important, right?”

“Yes amma. I will go and meet aunty after having these yummy pakoras.” Shakun did not intend to go but agreed, just to stop the conversation.

“Good. Take some for them when you go.” Amma insisted.

“What? No! Amma, please. That's not needed.”

“Why? It's the best way to pacify Jessy. And it’s our culture to share. You know that. So take this and go.” Amma smiled and handed over a tiffin box filled with hot pakoras for them.

Shakun rolled her eyes and took the box.

Sitting on the dining chair, Dad sipped his tea and listened to their conversation. He waved at Shakun as she walked past him, frowning, with the dabba in her hand.

Shakun had no choice now than to go to Jessy's house. She felt more anxious about meeting Abel than she did about Jessy. What if Jessy had already told him about her? What if he got angry with her? What if Jessy had told her mom too?

She hesitantly climbed down the stairs and walked past John's house. She tried to peek for John but, for some reason, did not wish to depend on him this time. She walked out of the gate and crossed over to Jessy's house.

18

She slowly opened the main door and looked in. All was quiet inside. She was not sure if she should call out for Jessy. She just stood there and was wondering what to do next when she heard Abel open the door and walk out of his room. Shakun wanted to turn and run away, but her legs felt glued to the floor. She stood there watching him walk towards her. She felt her heart would fall out of her chest. Abel looked unbelievably handsome in his red shirt with the question,'ready for love?' printed on it. She almost said yes to it but zipped her lips tight and waited. 'Does he know? Did Jessy tell him? God help me. Please,' she prayed.

"Shakun?? Hello, Dream Girl! When did you come?" Abel asked in a surprised tone.

Shakun smiled. She was relieved to hear him talk as normally as he always did. She smiled more broadly and revealed the box she was holding.

"Amma made. She told me to give it to you all too."

"Oh..wow! I was just wondering what to eat. Thank you."

"Where are Jessy and Aunty?"

"Shopping. I can have all of this." He pointed to the box and sat on the sofa smiling.

Shakun felt a thrill in her navel to be alone with Abel for the first time. She was filled with strange thoughts. She stood still not knowing what to do next. Should she go or...

"What happened? Come. sit."

Shakun was determined not to let go of this God-granted time of getting to be alone with him. She sat facing Abel and watched him relish the pakoras. She felt so drawn to him like some iron pieces to a magnet. His pink lips moved in circles, chewing the snack. Her eyes travelled down his throat when he swallowed the food. She allowed her mind to wander and dragged her eyes down his chest. She was jealous of the shirt that stuck to his skin. She could hug him tighter than that. She imagined sitting on his lap and popping the pakoras into his mouth. With her face so close to his, she could feel his breath, which had a scent of love in it. She smiled at him as he pushed away the strand of hair that was rubbing her cheek, then smiled back. Anyone who saw them would assume they were to kiss. But Abel snapped his fingers to bring her back to the present, shattering Shakun's imagination once again.

“Dreaming again? How are you able to do this?” Abel laughed.

Shakun felt embarrassed and changed the topic.

“John told me that both of you were going to meet Kavya. When is that?” Shakun spoke hurriedly. Abel’s smile faded. He looked at her with concern, wondering how much John had told her about Kavya.

“Eh, nothing is decided. In fact, I don't even know if I want to meet her.” He got up to wash his hands.

Shakun understood that he was uncomfortable discussing it. At the same time, she felt a small hope that Abel would stay away from Kavya, re-igniting her flames of love for him.

“I am sorry. I didn't mean to interfere.” She said it out loud to impress him.

“It’s ok. You just surprised me a little with that question. That's all.”

“John was quite upset today. So I forced him to tell me. He would not have told otherwise. Please don’t get frustrated with him for sharing it with me.” she continued

“No. That’s okay. I know you both are very close.”

Shakun felt the tickles in her tummy when Abel came back and sat next to her on the sofa, looking straight into her eyes. It was a quiet moment for both. Shakun observed Abel’s smile slowly fade away, and she saw a new passion in his eyes. He had never before looked so closely at her face. She sensed an unfamiliar intimacy that told her that Abel too was probably feeling drawn to her at that moment, like she was to him. Something changed, and something felt new. She saw him look deep into her eyes, and she longed for whatever would happen next.

“You have the most beautiful eyes I have ever seen. Like two fishes facing each other.” Abel said in a dazzled tone.

Shakun could feel the excitement grow within her. She let him look deeper into her eyes. If that could make him forget Kavya forever. But…

“I'm sure they are not as lovely as Kavya's,” she said, not knowing how else to respond. She immediately felt stupid for reminding Abel of exactly the same thing that she did not want him to think of. Foolish girl, she thought to herself.

Abel smiled. “I'm not sure about Kavya. What do you think I should do, Shakun?” he said softly, not looking away.

Shakun wondered why she felt her name sounded sweeter when it came out of Abel's mouth. He now sat so close to her that she could see herself in his marble-brown eyes. She felt intoxicated by his looks, and her throat went dry of words.

"What about... Abel?". She managed to push the words out.

"Do you think I should forgive Kavya?". Abel asked while his eyes swayed from side to side, looking deep into hers. This was the first time that Shakun sat so near to him. His breath blew onto her face, and she felt her soul melt into it. Shakun loved this closeness. She could see the open pores on his skin, which were releasing tiny strands of moustache hair above his lips. She wished that the moment froze forever. She was tempted to hold his face in her hands and make him look at the love that was brimming in her eyes.

Shakun was quiet. She preferred to just be close to him rather than answer him.

"Tell me... Shakun? What would you do if you were me?" he whispered. Shakun felt caught in that question. She didn't dare look away from his eyes.

"There is someone better waiting for you. Someone who will love you as much as you deserve," she said.

Abel immediately remembered that John had told him the same thing. "There is someone better for you."

The room was filled with silence. Both of them gazed into each other for a long time. Abel's eyes tried to read the expression of her eyes. Something told Shakun that he liked what she had just told. His eyes slowly scrolled down from her eyes to her lips, and Shakun knew what was coming up. Abel moved closer to Shakun's lips. An unexpected fear leaped inside her, and she broke the silence.

“How does all this matter to you anyway? You will be leaving soon for America, right?”

She muttered. Abel listened to her words without making any movement.

“Yes, I wanted to. But now... I am not sure,” he whispered, slowly returning to kiss her when the main door opened with a squeaky noise that shook them out of their private space. Both instantly moved away from each other to different corners of the sofa. They paused and realised the warmth in the air around them.

Abel took a deep sigh and ran to the door to help his mother walk in.

“Shakun has been waiting for you, Fatty." Abel said casually to his sister and helped his mom walk in. Jessy looked straight ahead at her friend seated on the sofa. Shakun tried to lock eyes with her, but Jessy ignored her.

“Hello aunty. How was the shopping?” Shakun came running to greet Abel’s mom. Jessy looked at her with the same anger that she had when she left John's room a few hours ago.

“Jessy wanted to buy some clothes. She was so upset for God knows what. And she wanted to shop to feel better. Get me some water, Abel.” Aunty said to Abel, looking tired. ‘God knows, and I know for sure too,’ Shakun thought.

Shakun’s eye followed Abel, who disappeared into the kitchen. Jessy noticed and stared suspiciously at Shakun. She walked past to her room and closed the door. Shakun took the insult.

“Ok aunty. I will come later. Bye.” Shakun quickly turned to walk out when Abel came back with water. They almost clashed on each other and exchanged glances that now felt uncomfortable.

“Bye, Abel.” She softly blew the words. Abel smiled shyly and waved bye.

Shakun walked to her home with such grace that she felt like she was floating on the ground. She could not believe what had happened. She ascended the stairs and sat on Winny's lap. She rested her head on Winny and whispered, ‘It happened, Winny. We almost kissed. I think Abel likes me.’ She pressed her cheek against Winny and hugged her. ‘I love you, Winny. But not as much as Abel,’ she giggled and walked directly towards her room. Amma watched her walk into her room. She called out for her, but Shakun went in and closed the door behind her. She fell onto her bed, facing the fan above, and closed her eyes. She relived the moments when Abel and she were close to each other. It felt magical to have his eyes looking deep into her soul. She now felt a little guilty for stopping him. If only Jessy and Aunty had arrived two minutes later, she would have experienced the biggest mystery of her life. She replayed those minutes in her mind again and again. She began to feel a tickle in her stomach. Her closed eyes told her that it was Abel’s soft hand touching her, feeling her breath go up and down her belly. She felt the tickle slowly move upwards to her chest. STOP!! She opened her eyes wide and sat up sweating. There was no one in her room. She placed her hand on her stomach and smiled. Her excitement knew no bounds, and she grabbed her pillow, buried her face deep into it, and screamed. ‘I LOVE YOU, Abel... I LOVE YOU SO MUCH.’

19

The next morning Shakun woke up later than usual and heard people's voices from the living room. She opened her door and peered towards the hall. John's dad was seated on the bamboo chair and her dad on the plastic chair near him. Shakun immediately sensed a serious conversation taking place and wondered if it had anything to do with her.

"But this is so sudden, Mr. Robert? How can we?" Shakun heard her dad talking.

Shakun saw her mom in the kitchen, making tea for the guest. She joined in and noticed she was worried.

"Amma..what happened? Why has uncle come here?" Shakun whispered

"They want us to vacate this house."

"What? Why?" Her voice was loud.

"Ssshhhh… will tell you when he leaves. Go and take a bath. It's so late already."

"No. You tell me now. Bath can wait."

"Mr. Richard wants his brother and family to move in here so they can all stay together," she said, irritated.

"But what about us, then? Where do we go?"

"I don't know Ammu. You go now. They are waiting for tea." Amma carried the tea tray to the hall.

Shakun felt shattered. She cannot go away from Abel. Definitely not now, when she was just winning his love. Nothing else was her concern. Not John, not Jessy... Just Abel.

“They will come only by the end of this month. You still have time to find yourself a new place. And I will also help you find one.” Shakun heard Mr. Robert say this as she made her way back to her room.

Shakun locked herself in and banged her fist on the wall.

“No no no… This is not fair, Gannu. You cannot do this to me.” She said, pointing at the little Ganesha idol kept on her study table.

Shakun stood perplexed, unable to believe what she heard from Mr. Robert. However, she was confident that her father would handle the situation and they would not leave this place. After all, her dad was her superman who could solve all her problems. Shakun relaxed and went for her shower. After taking a refreshingly cold shower, Shakun dressed to look her best for Abel, should she happen to run into him. She walked to the dining table; she saw her dad and mom waiting for her quietly. She pulled up a chair and served the idlis for herself. She noticed that both of their plates were empty, so she filled them too. They appeared lost in thought. Shakun coughed pretentiously to bring them back to the present.

“Appa, don't worry. I think Uncle will come again to tell us that it won’t be necessary.” Shakun seemed too sure about it.

“No Ammu. He won’t. We have to start searching for another house.” He was serious this time.

"But... but..Appa. I don't want to go too far away from school," she reasoned, as if it mattered at all.

"And away from Abel." Her heart screamed out loud.

"We'll try to find a house nearby. Mr. Robert has promised to help," he said as he ate.

Shakun now felt hopeless, and it scared her.

"Appa, I have my best friends here," she tried again soberly.

"We are not leaving the country, dear. You can come here to meet them whenever you wish.

And I am sure you will find new friends there too." This time Appa was firm.

"I love this house, Appa." She gave him her last shot of emotional attack.

"Listen Shakun. Your mom and I too are attached to this place. But we have to accept the change that life demands." Appa was loud and left the dining area without finishing his food.

Shakun was shocked to see her father get frustrated with her. It never happened before. She stared at her mother, who looked at her helplessly.

Shakun washed her hands and locked herself in her room. She could not believe that her love story would end so abruptly even before it started. Since the day they moved to Madras, there has not been a single day that she has not seen Abel. He had become an inseparable part of her life. And now, all of a sudden, she will be gone, leaving her heart behind. Forever. She could not control her anguish and sobbed into her pillow.

It did not help her control her sorrow. She ran down to meet John.

“He is not here, Shakun,” his mom said, opening the door.

“Is he at Abel’s place?”

"He said they would both be meeting another friend. They didn’t tell me who.”

Shakun knew for sure it was Kavya. She felt betrayed that Abel had finally returned to Kavya, despite the events of the previous evening. Nobody seemed to care for her. Not John, not Jessy. not Appa, not Amma, not anybody!!

Shakun was so angry that she hurried to Jessy’s house to talk face-to-face with her. She wanted her friend back. She opened their main door and saw Jessy’s mom rushing out of the kitchen, wiping her tears with her saree pillow. Something seemed wrong.

20

"Aunty, what happened?"

Abel's mom turned back and looked at her in despair. "It's Jessy. It happened again," she said with a choked voice as she ran into Jessy's room.

Shakun's eyes widened, and tears filled in. She ran behind aunty to Jessy's room. She felt the shock of her life to see Jessy's whole body shaking with uncontrollable movements and saliva foaming out from the corner of her mouth. Her eyes were rolled up, and her hands and legs stiffened out with her head pressed to the side of the pillow. Aunty assisted Abel and John in turning her body to the side to allow the froth to flow out smoothly. Shakun had, a few months ago, heard from John about Jessy's seizures, but this was the first time she actually witnessed it. She quickly picked a towel from Jessy's wardrobe and stood near her head. They waited for her body to calm down on its own. Jessy's seizure caused her to bite her own lower lip so deeply that it swelled up and oozed blood from the corners of her mouth. Shakun placed the towel under Jessy's cheek to soak the blood and her foamy saliva. All stood helplessly with fear until the seizure ceased. Jessy's body slowly loosened and relaxed. Her tired body nullified her to sleep, and her face now looked less scary with her purple blood-clotted, swollen lip. Shakun slowly wiped the froth and blood off her mouth and cheeks, then placed her head straight on the pillow. Aunty drew a cross over her chest and rushed to her prayer room to express her gratitude to her Lord Jesus. Shakun looked up at Abel and John. She saw both hassled in fear. She looked at Abel, who was still staring at his sister, unable to comprehend what had just happened. She watched him struggle to control himself. She slowly walked over to John and whispered to him to take Abel out of there. John nodded and pulled Abel out of the room. As Shakun watched them walk out together, she hoped and prayed that John would be able to help Abel handle himself.

At John's home, Abel ran and crashed on to John's bed, covered his face with a pillow, and wailed loudly. John quickly followed and closed his door behind him. He sat beside Abel, letting him cry. Abel sobbed into the pillow till it drained out some of his pain. There was silence in the room, and John rubbed his back to console him. Abel wiped his tears and sat down, leaning against the bedside with his hands resting on his folded knees. He rubbed his nose on his sleeves and breathed long sighs. John sat on the bed, facing him. He held Abel's palm and stroked it quietly. No questions asked. Many minutes passed until the silence helped Abel compose himself. Abel looked at John with puffy eyes, and tears began to layer again. John instantly knew what was hitting Abel's head.

"Don't ask yourself too many questions, Abel. We don't know why it happened again, after so many years."

Abel shook his head in agreement without uttering a word.

"I will get you some water." John held Abel's face up and smiled to distract him. He started to get up when Abel pulled him back down and hugged him tight.

"I got so scared, John. I had just gone to wake her up. That's all. She abruptly collapsed and began trembling. I don't remember the last time it happened. It felt so new, and I did not know what to do." Abel hid his head on John's shoulders and cried again.

John pulled Abel's face away from his shoulder and looked into his watery eyes.

“I know you got scared, Abel. And it's okay to get scared too.”

"But how could she get it when she has been taking medicines regularly? Why did she get it? I need to know that, John.”

The question struck John like lightning, and he instantly knew what had shaken Jessy so much to trigger her long-subsided epilepsy. John stood perplexed.

“The last time it happened was when your dad left for the US 5 years ago. The very next morning. Don't you remember?”

“Yes. Now I do. She never wanted dad to go. She was so upset that day.“ Abel paused and continued with intrigue. “But why now, John? What could upset her so much?”

Though John knew the answer, he did not think it was the right time for honesty.

"Seizures do not require a reason for their trigger, Abel." They just occur. Jessy is also very sensitive. Maybe something upset her, and you can ask her when she is better. Am sure she would know.”

He calmed down a little and said, "Hmm..I will."

"Where’s Uncle and Aunty?" Abel asked, looking around.

“Mommy must be cooking. Dad left for church. Some discussion on charity work. Come! Let’s go and see how your dear sister is doing now. Also, don't cry in front of her. Ok?” John punched Abel in the stomach, and they both walked back to Abel's house.

21

Abel and John entered Jessy's room and found her still asleep. They stood at the door, and Abel's eye caught Shakun sitting on a chair near Jessy. Her hands gently patted Jessy's forehead to comfort her. Shakun's round face glowed under the bright sunlight that swept into the room through the open window. He gazed at her long, curly hair, which hung loosely down to her waist. Just then, a strand of hair flew forward, brushing her cheek and got stuck between her rosy lips. Shakun swiped her fingers over her cheek, pulling the strand away and tucking it behind her ears. Abel smiled to himself as he felt a strange tingle in his heart. He thought of the previous evening, when he had for the first time looked deep into her eyes and wondered how he had missed noticing such a beauty right next door. And now he felt a new wave of attraction towards her. Abel struggled to focus on Jessy while his eyes kept rolling back to Shakun, who sat there like an angel guarding his sister. Abel tightly clenched his fists and closed his eyes, resisting the urge to lift her up and give her a passionate kiss. Such things never happened with Kavya. He heard his heart scream at him. 'This is love, Abel. You have fallen in love with Shakun.' He ran his hand over his hair and clenched his fists in excitement. John noticed his unusual behaviour and tapped his shoulder inquisitively.

"Are you ok?" he whispered into Abel's ears.

"I am not sure, John. It's Shakun. I think I am falling in love with her," he replied softly.

John looked at Abel and smiled in agreement. He squeezed Abel's hands and whispered back, "Maybe she is the one for you."

Abel looked at him and then turned to Shakun. She now sat beside Jessy with a towel in her hand. She wiped Jessy's forehead to cool down the fever that had risen during the seizure. Jessy slowly opened her eyes and looked at her best friend. She immediately sat up, pushing Shakun's hand away, and smiled at Abel, who rushed towards her. John noticed Shakun sadly moving away to let the siblings have their moment.

“How are you now, fatty?” Abel casually teased his sister.

“Just tired.” Jessy replied in a low voice.

“Mmm..come here.” Abel opened his arms, and Jessy crawled into it for his warm, tight hug.

“Are YOU okay?” Jessy surprised her brother with that question.

Abel faced his sister and smiled.

“Of course. Why?”

"I can tell by your face that you've cried. I know I scared you.” Jessy said apologetically.

Abel shook his head, denying her.

“Let's go to the doctor in the evening,” he said, feeling responsible. His mother walked in with rice and soup, saying,

“Not necessary, Abel! I have given her the medicine. There is nothing more to do. She just needs more rest," Aunty hinted to all of them to leave.

Abel kissed his sister on the head and walked out of the room, with John following him.

Watching Abel's affection for his sister made Shakun's heart grow so much fonder of him. Every time she saw him, she knew she loved him an inch deeper than before. She felt her legs go weak as she saw him walk away. She struggled to stay composed and focussed on Jessy.

"Aunty, can I stay here with Jessy for some more time? Please?" Shakun shifted her thoughts and asked politely

"NO..I don't want anybody here." Jessy intruded.

Jessy's angry tone brought Shakun back to the present situation.

"Jessy… Don't be so rude to her. You don't know how much she was worried for you. She took care of you when you were unconscious. She cleaned and changed your clothes too. You better be nice to her," Aunty scolded, leaving the room.

Shakun stayed back and waited for Jessy to speak. Jessy sat leaning on the bedside with her head down, meddling with her fingers. Shakun walked over and sat down beside Jessy. She slowly placed her palm on Jessy's restless hands and squeezed them. Jessy looked up, and tears filled in. She quickly moved forward to hug Shakun tightly and sobbed her heart out. Shakun hugged her back and cried in happiness. She realised how much she will miss Jessy when she leaves this neighbourhood.

Jessy broke the silence and spoke.

"I am sorry, Shakun. What you said yesterday was such a shock for me. I just felt awful and confused about it. But I know that I have no right to stop you from loving anyone. Even if that happens to be my own brother." Jessy hid her face in Shakun's neck and cried.

From behind, Shakun stroked Jessy's hair and kissed her head.

"I will never do anything to hurt you, Jessy. You are my only best friend, and I love you very much."

Shakun held Jessy's face in her hands and said firmly

"It's true that I love him dearly. But you are more important to me, Jessy. If you do not like it, then I promise I will try to let go of Abel. I will slowly forget him. But I cannot see you suffer like this again." Shakun choked.

"No no. Shakun, you don't have to do anything like that. What else is better than to see my best friend and my brother together? And I never liked Kavya, anyway! I will tell Abel that you love him so much more than that idiot Kavya," Jessy giggled.

"NO…Jessy! Please do not tell him anything. I have decided to face my fears and talk to him directly about everything from now on. Promise me that you won't." Shakun opened her palms for Jessy.

"I don't understand you sometimes. Fine. Promise." She placed her hand on Shakun's to validate her words.

"But you better tell him fast. He is planning to go to the US very soon. You know that, right?"

"Yes." Shakun shook her head sadly.

“Oh ho… Don’t be sad. Even if he goes, he will come back soon. He cannot be without seeing me or Mummy. So you don't worry at all.”

Shakun smiled in relief. She could not believe that she had gotten back her best friend and hugged her tight in excitement.

For a minute, Shakun had forgotten about her moving out of the neighbourhood, and now it hit her hard.

Shakun freed herself from Jessy’s hug and looked straight into her eyes.

“But I am not lucky to be with your brother, Jessy.”

“Eh, what?’

“We will be vacating this house by the end of this month.”

Jessy’s eyes widened.

“Why? What happened, and where are you shifting to?” Jessy was non-stop with her questions.

"Uncle's brother and family wish to stay here together. So we have to move out.”

"But what about us? What about John and Abel?"

“I don't know how I am going to live without you all, Jessy.”

“Mmm...we all or without Abel?” Jessy winked at her teasingly

Shakun smiled shyly, knowing how true that was.

“Don’t worry, Shakun. Wherever we are, we will meet in school every day.”

“Yes. But I won't be able to see...” Shakun stopped before finishing.

“My brother…eh? Maybe he won't go at all if you tell him that you looovvve him.” Jessy dragged the word love, miming it with a funny face.

“Why? Has he ever told you anything about me?” Shakun asked curiously.

“Maybe.”

“Really? Jessy, tell me... please..please" Shakun begged with folded hands.

"Hey, hey. Calm down. In fact, he has never spoken to me about you except for once.”

“And what was that about?”

“He told me that he had teased you when he saw your unbuttoned shirt and wanted me to say sorry to you on his behalf. I refused. But it's true that he felt very guilty for that unacceptable behaviour.”

Shakun hit her own forehead with her hand and sighed in embarrassment.

"And yes, he once told me that the Dream girl is becoming more and more beautiful every day.Nothing more than that. I swear.” Jessy pinched her throat.

Shakun smiled wide and kissed Jessy on her cheeks.

“Thank you, my darling. I love you.”

Shakun felt that she could live her whole life just remembering these words.

“You look as fresh as a lotus now, dear.” Jessy’s mom smiled at her daughter as she walked in with more food for her.

Shakun got up from Jessy’s bed.

“Shall I get you some lunch, Shakun?”

"No, thank you, Aunty. I was just leaving.” Shakun smiled wider at Aunty. She turned to Jessy, waved her a bye, and walked towards their gate. She found John and Abel standing there, talking about something seriously. She remembered that moment when Abel wanted to kiss her, and she again felt a chill on her lips. As she passed by them, she noticed that they instantly stopped talking, whatever it was. Shakun pretended not to notice and spoke casually.

“Are you feeling better, Abel?” She managed to look into his eyes and speak.

“Yes…why?” Abel asked, pretending to be cool.

“Just like that. I imagined you crying...like a baby.’ she giggled, teasing him.

Abel’s face turned red, and he held her upper arm tight with anger and pulled her close to him. He never liked anyone teasing him or his sister.

Shakun and Abel faced each other closely once again, but this time she did not see love in his eyes. There was no passion, no urge, no mystery in his looks. Just plain anger.

John interfered and forced Abel to let go of his grip on Shakun's arm.

"Abel…stop it. She was just joking. What's wrong with you?" John pulled Abel aside.

Shakun stood still, aghast at his behaviour.

"You go home, Shakun." John pushed her away, pointing to their home across the street.

Shakun walked away with her head down, not knowing what had just happened.

She climbed up the stairs and sat on Winny's lap. She looked down at Abel, who was still there, looking disturbed.

"Do you see him, Winny? Why did he suddenly get so upset with me?" Winny just silently watched it all.

Shakun kept looking down at Abel. She wanted him to look up at her. She knew he would, if he was sorry for what he did. She waited. She started to count, just like in the movies. 1...2...6.....8…9…and Abel looked up at her with eyes of guilt and shame. Shakun felt overwhelmed, but she controlled herself and waited for his response. John stood near him, looking elsewhere, pretending not to be a part of the show at all. Abel held both his ears with his hands and mimed 'sorry' through the air. He pretended to slap himself for his mistake. Shakun could no longer hold on to her grudge, and she smiled wide at him. Abel laughed with her, and John joined the fun.

Shakun was still smiling wide when she noticed Abel's smile slowly fade away and his eyes move to her side. Shakun turned and saw her father standing beside her, looking down at Abel. She instantly felt her stomach cramp in fear. Appa looked at her with anger. Shakun sensed that everything will come to an end soon.

22

"Go inside." Appa ordered. "NOW". He shouted.

Shakun ran in, trembling. She locked herself in her room, afraid to face him anymore.

Amma saw her running and came knocking on her door.

"What happened, Ammu?"

"Nothing happened. You set the table for lunch. I will bring her." Appa replied harshly.

Amma had never witnessed her husband becoming upset with their daughter before. She knew it was not the time to ask anything more. She quietly followed his instruction.

Appa knocked on Shakun's door.

"Shakun, come for lunch." Appa spoke calmly, then walked away to the dining area.

Shakun sat on her bed, remembering how much her dad had started to dislike Abel for all the fights he did on the streets. Appa once caught Abel using foul language. He came home complaining about Abel's behaviour and warned Shakun not to have any friendship with him. Though he was fine with Jessy coming over every single day, he hated Abel for his street brawls. And now he had seen the same boy act funny with his daughter.

Shakun knew that a bomb would blast at the dining table. She opened the door and joined him, while Amma restlessly placed the dishes.

“Look Shakun..” Appa just started when

“Appa…wait. I want to talk first this time.” Shakun interrupted boldly.

“I know you don’t like Abel. I know that you think he is a brat. You think he is a spoilt boy. You think he is indisciplined and ill-mannered. But you know what? He is nothing that you think he is. Do you remember when he came here with John to help us with my admission? At that time, you had mentioned to him that he possessed a generous heart. He is still that same boy, Appa.”

Appa and Amma remained dumbstruck, while Shakun let go of herself and continued to talk for Abel.

"Do you know why he fights with his friends? Because he cannot forgive anyone who hurts his mom or sister. He is such a responsible and caring person, Appa. He does everything for them that his dad would have done if he were here. Abel does his dad’s duties, Appa. And you just hate him without knowing any truth. That is wrong. He is also my best friend, along with John and Jessy. And I am very fond of him too.” Shakun slowed down and took a long breath. She gently placed her hand on Appa’s wrist. “He is a wonderful boy, Appa, and that’s why he is everyone’s hero. Mine too.” Shakun stopped and waited. Either to be slapped or scolded by him.

Amma stared at Shakun with an open mouth, unable to let all the words seep into her head. Appa continued to eat quietly. Minutes passed until he broke the silence.

“Get ready to forget all of them. We will be moving out of this place in 2 weeks.” Appa finished his meal and left the table.

23

Fearing his sister might get another attack of the seizure, Abel spent the rest of the day with her. Though John had reminded him about meeting Kavya, he dared not leave his sister's side. Kavya can wait. Like how he had waited, not so long ago.

"Why are you sticking with me like this, Abel? It's already 5. It's time for your evening gang meeting. Not going?"

"No. It's no big deal. I can meet them tomorrow."

"Offoo… I am FINE, my dear brother. If that's what's keeping you from going, I understand. Mom is here anyway. Go and have fun."

"Mom wants me to be home." Abel said, looking at his sister with concern.

"Poor thing, she kept pretending to be strong, but I saw her in the kitchen, breathlessly sobbing. I won't leave you both to yourselves." he finished.

"Oh, really? So what will happen when you join dad? Who will sit here like this for us, eh?" Jessy reminded him with a tease.

"Who said I am going?" Abel asked calmly.

"What do you mean? You are not going? Why? Because of me? My sickness?" Jessy sat up, straight-tailing one question after the other.

Abel held her shoulders and waited for her to stop.

"It's not just about you. I don't think it's as important for me to go as being here with you and mom. I have already told her, and I will tell dad too when he calls tonight. I am sure he will appreciate my decision."

"But...what about your college? Your future?" Jessy became emotional.

"I will join a good one here. Nothing to worry about."

Jessy's eyes filled with love, and she hugged him tight.

"I am sorry, Abel." She sobbed.

Abel gently touched her head.

"Ssshhhh….it's ok. It was not your fault. But why do you think you had a seizure? Did anything happen that upset you? Or did anyone hurt you?" Abel took the chance to ask her.

"This Shakun... she is the reason for everything." Jessy broke the embrace and faced her brother.

"Shakun? Why? What did she do?" Abel was taken by surprise to hear her name.

"Yes. She is the one. She gave me this shocking news. She said, "Sshhee... Jessy stopped. She remembered the promise she had made to Shakun that she would never tell Abel about her love for him. She stared into her brother's eyes, confused about what to say next.

"She what? What did she say, Jessy? Tell me.? Abel urged her.

"She said..she. She is shifting. Yes. She is moving out of here. Yes. That's what she said. And I could not bear that. She is my bestie, and it shocked me." Jessy blurted the truth. But not the real truth.

Abel stared into his sister's eyes. He felt a sudden vacuum in his heart. It felt like something heavy had been removed. "Why am I feeling sad? I never felt so empty, even when Kavya left me. Then why now? What is happening?" Abel's heart confused him.

"Abel…? What happened?" Jessy shook him.

"Shakun is shifting. That's it? And for THAT, you had a seizure?" Abel acted out the drama, rolling his eyes.

Jessy gave a blank smile.

"I don't know Abel. I just know I was disturbed. That's how I am. Too sensitive."

"Oh my God!! You are mad. And where is she shifting to? To London?" Abel mocked.

"No…no..not out of India." Jessy laughed loudly. "It should only be somewhere near school."

Abel couldn't accept this absurd explanation for her seizure. It was definitely something else, but he did not wish to bother her anymore. He held her face in his hands with affection.

"Even if the whole world moves away from you, I will never leave your side." Abel said, while his eyes filled with tears of love.

"I know. I have the best brother in the world."

Mommy watched them quietly from the doorside and crossed her heart, thanking Jesus for blessing her with such lovely children.

24

It was a little after sunset. John rushed to meet Abel.

“Aunty, where is he?” he asked Abel’s mom, who was lighting candles for prayer.

“To buy bread...from Naadaar’s,” she replied without getting distracted.

John ran towards the bakery at the street corner. It did not even occur to him to check on Jessy. He was half way there when he saw Abel walking back with his purchases. His gasp for breath frightened Abel.

“John… Why are you running like this? What happened? Is it Jessy again?” he trembled.

John shook his head to say "no" as he began to breathe slower.

“Kavya… She tried suicide. We need to go. NOW.”

“What? Stop blabbering, John.” Abel stammered

“Come….let’s GOOOO…” John shouted. Abel understood something terrible had happened. They ran back to Abel's house. He handed over the groceries to his mom and dragged out his dusty red bike.

“Where are you both going?” Aunty screamed from inside.

“Will be back soon” was the only reply she got.

“Where are we going now?" Abel asked, starting his bike.

“To her house.”

“Are you going to tell me what happened?” Abel lost his patience and screamed through his helmet.

“Kavya’s housemaid came home some half an hour back. She said Kavya cut her wrist and tried to kill herself this afternoon.”

“Oh my god!! But why? And how is she now? Did her maid tell you?”

“No. Let’s go find out. Go faster”

As they reached her gate, Abel remembered all those good days when he had dropped her off from school and how they exchanged love talks and flying kisses before she had walked in. He felt guilty for avoiding her when she wanted to meet him. She probably needed help and wouldn't have taken such a drastic step otherwise. His thoughts took a rally, and he hurriedly parked the bike, and they together ran to her house on the second floor. Abel rang the bell and waited.

A minute passed, and Abel noticed John trembling in fear. He knew that John still loved her and had pretended to have given up on her for his own sake. But now, his love was so obvious in his teary eyes.

“She will be ok, John.” Abel tapped his shoulder. Just then he realised he had no more romantic feelings for Kavya.

John looked at him with surprise and slowly smiled. Everything else was untold and understandable.

And then suddenly, someone opened the door. It was Kiran. Kavya’s 9-year-old little brother.

They barged in, pushing him aside.

“Where is she?” Abel searched.

John leaned down, shook little Kiran, and repeated his question. “Where is she? Is she ok?”

“In her room,” Kiran pointed up.

“Why is the house so quiet? Where are your parents?” John asked curiously.

“I don't know.” Kiran shrugged his shoulders and ran back to watch TV.

Abel and John exchanged glances with confusion.

They looked up and climbed the steps in a rush. They banged the door open and found Kavya standing near her window, looking outside. They were surprised to see her fit, while they expected to see her lying unconscious on her bed with her parents sitting on both sides with sad faces.

“Abel…” She turned and ran towards Abel, giving him a tight hug. She held his face with both of her palms and kissed him all over.

“What are you doing?” Abel pushed her away. He was more irritated with her than relieved to see her well.

“What’s all this, Kavya? Your maid came home and told me..” John asked with wonder,

“I know... I know... She told you that I cut my wrist and tried to kill myself. I know. I gave her 100 rupees as her fee for that.” Kavya completed.

"What the hell is happening?" John was furious this time.

Kavya ignored John and spoke to Abel.

"Abel ... I did not know how else to see you. I am sorry I lied. But I now know that I love you, Abel. "I want us back together," Kavya said hysterically, holding his collar.

Abel lost his nerve and grabbed her by the hair.

"Aaahhh..." she screamed in pain.

"No..Abel..don't!" John warned.

Abel pulled her hair and squeezed it tighter. He hadn't yet forgiven her for playing with his love. He pulled her closer.

"You are right. I did love you with all my heart. But not anymore. And I never will." Abel said angrily.

Kavya pulled his hands away from her hair and slowly smiled.

"You know what? You are a liar, Abel. You cannot live without me because I am the only one you love. Only me..the most beautiful of all..KAVYA!! She said, pointing to herself.

Abel stood shocked to see this new ugly side of her. John saw that Abel was losing his temper again, and before he could charge at her, John interfered.

"Don't you dare talk to him like that. He is no longer your toy to play with and discard after you finish. I'm sure you did the same to Arun. Didn't you?" John asked

"Arun..? That idiot? He was so boring," she said in despair.

John and Abel exchanged looks in disbelief. Abel walked to Kavya.

"Look Kavya. I don't care about you or Arun. But it's over between you and me. I am not in love with you anymore. So... Goodbye."

"Oh... does that mean there is someone else now? ...Eh? " Kavya asked mockingly.

Abel stared into Kavya's eyes, and his heart suddenly popped Shakun's face to his mind, and he froze with a new realisation. John looked at Abel and waited.

"Yes," Abel said softly. The room filled with silence. Kavya stared at Abel, hoping that it was all a joke, and he would burst out laughing and hug her back in happiness. But that did not happen. Kavya knew her karma was giving her the returns of a lifetime.

Meanwhile, John now felt very sure of something that he had wanted to do since the time Kavya had broken his best friend's heart. He walked to the couple and moved Abel away from Kavya. He stood facing her and stared into her eyes which he had once found most beautiful. Just as Kavya started to speak, "Phat!" John slapped her hard across the face. "I should have done this long back, bitch!" he said angrily. While Kavya took her time to understand what had happened, John turned back to Abel and dragged him out of the house.

The ride back home was a quiet one till they reached home. John jumped off the bike and looked at Abel.

"What happened to you there, John?" Abel asked.

"Nothing. She deserved it for treating you the way she did. That's all." John said calmly.

"Wow.. I don't know what to say. Thank you." Abel became emotional.

"Ah, drama king! By the way, I liked what you told Kavya. You confessed your love for someone else. I believe that is Shakun. Right? John asked with a doubt in his tone. Abel paused and smiled.

"What do you think?" he said, winking.

"I think what you think." John replied with a smile. He winked back and gave a friendly punch to Abel before disappearing into his house. Abel parked his bike and walked in when he realised something. He took a step back and looked up at Winny. Shakun stood there, looking down at him. The moonlight shone on her face, and she looked like an angel waiting for him. The tender breeze blew her hair away from her face, and he felt his eyes stuck to it. He waved at her and smiled. Something told him that she had been there for a long time. Waiting for him. He walked in still confused if she was the real 'Someone' in his life now.

"Where were you, Abel?" Jessy asked, running to the door.

"Why, what happened, fatty?" Abel pinched her cheeks as he came in.

"Daddy had called Naadaar uncle's number. He wanted to talk to you. Then mommy went and spoke."

"Anything special?" Abel asked as he washed his feet near the tap under their mango tree.

“Daddy wants all of us to move to the US...not just you,” she said sadly.

“What? But why now? You need to finish your 12th grade.” Abel asked in confusion.

“Daddy is worried about Jessy’s health. He wants us to be together now. He says she will get better treatment there,” his mother replied from the kitchen.

“But...when is he expecting us to go?” he asked

“End of this month. Since we already have our passports, visas will be easy.”

“This month? That is only 2 weeks from now, mummy?”

“Yes..”

Abel immediately thought of Shakun. It had been just a few hours when he realised his love for her. He was sure that he did not wish to go away from her. Not now.

“But what about this house, mummy? We can't just lock it up and go,” he said, hoping that it would in some way change the situation.

“He told me to talk to your aunt and hand over the keys to her when we leave. She can rent it later.”

Abel stood quiet with his hands on his hips, thinking about Shakun and feeling hopeless.

“I will miss Shakun a lot,” Jessy said as if she heard Abel’s thoughts.

"Mmm... me too," he said, before realising that he said it aloud. He bit his tongue and hoped Jessy had not heard him.

"What? Why would YOU miss her?" Jessy said.

Abel looked at her and tried to sound normal.

"I will miss all my friends here, Jessy. And that includes her too."

Jessy looked suspiciously deep into his eyes, as if searching for some new meaning in what he had just said.

"Mummy… Did Daddy say when he was arranging our tickets?" He shouted to divert Jessy's thoughts.

"30th of this month. 2 a.m. flight. There is a lot of work before we lock this house down."

25

It was a long, sleepless night for Shakun. She rolled over and glanced at the small square clock on her study table. It told her 1 a.m. 'Is your battery dying, clocky? Why are you not moving faster?' She spoke angrily to her tiny pink clock.

She held the piece in her hand and spoke to it. 'Sorry. I just can't sleep. The minute I close my eyes, I only see his face. I fear leaving this place, clocky. What if he forgets me? What if he finds someone else?' Shakun looked at it pointlessly. 'That's not your problem anyway.' She placed it back hard on the table. She got out of bed and walked out of her room quietly in her long-night gown. She slowly opened the main door and stared at Winny. She walked on toes towards her favourite place, one step at a time. She saw the moon right in front of her. She stood amazed by the beauty of it. A huge, full moon, like a big white ball, stuck to the clean, spotless blue sky, seeping its white light smoothly through Winny. The chill moonlight lit the entire verandah. She placed her hands on Winny and felt the cold metal wake up with her touch.

Shakun sat leaning her back against Winny's side wall, looking out. She was mesmerised by the beauty of the night. She wondered how this tender night queen could so easily defeat the day's ruling sun. She felt sad that she had only a few more days to sit here like this, on Winny's lap, and gaze up into the skies. Nowhere in the whole wide world can she find a place like this. A place that her heart had gotten stuck to. A place that gave her the best memories of friendship and love. A place that taught her to see beyond faces and admire the beauty in people's hearts.

Through the swaying leaves of their mango tree, Shakun looked down at Abel's house. The thought of going away from Abel pinched her heart once again. She secretly wished that he, too, walked out of his room, unable to sleep. She tapped her head and smiled to herself for dreaming of such impossible things. She was sure he was in bed, totally unaware of her turmoil. Just when she thought to go back to her room, she saw Abel walking in the dark towards his gate. She rubbed her eyes in disbelief. Of late, God seemed to listen to all her wishes and grant them generously, considering her last days here. Fair enough!!

Abel slowly opened the gate and stepped out, closing it behind him. He glanced at both sides of the lane and sat down, folding his legs. Shakun observed him fiddling with his hands, a behaviour he typically exhibits when deeply troubled by something. She felt the urge to wave at him but stopped herself for some reason. 'Look up, Abel... here... it's me...' She said softly to herself.

The wind heard her words and blew so hard on the leaves on the ground that one of them landed on Abel's face. He tossed his head upwards to brush the leaf away, and his eyes fell on Shakun. He slowly stood up, not moving his eyes from her face. He wanted to take some more time to understand if he was actually seeing her or if he was just hallucinating. Shakun, not knowing what else to do, waved gently at Abel and smiled. Yes. She was there, for real.

Abel smiled and waved back. Shakun's eyes filled with tears of joy. She had nothing more to ask from God. She waited. Abel took courage and spoke with his hands. He pointed at her and mimed, "Come down." Shakun understood his action and waved both her hands for a "no.".

Abel folded his hands and begged. “Plleeeaaaseee…”

Though she was scared to her neck, she did not wish to let go of this time. After all, it was God’s will. She shook her head and mimed back. ”I am coming.” She went back and peeped into her house. No movement anywhere. She could hear her parents snore in turns. She slowly closed the door from outside and climbed down the stairs. John’s house was also quiet. It meant Mr. Robert was not home to snore. She walked past their door and toward the gate. She saw Abel already there. Her legs trembled in fear. It was the first time that she was doing something so dangerous. She asked God for one last thing. Let the whole world sleep forever.

She reached the gate and smiled at Abel. They stood facing each other, with the gate in between. Neither of them believed what was happening. They stood looking at each other in silence. Abel broke the trance and checked if he could open the gate. Shakun stopped him and showed the lock that was hanging down. John always locked the gate at night. Shakun shook her head and whispered. “It's locked.”

Abel smiled at her. “It’s okay,” he whispered back. “Why are you awake, dream girl?” Abel asked. Shakun loved it whenever he called her that way.

“I couldn’t sleep. I don't know why,” she said. “And you?”

“Same. Was not feeling sleepy at all.”

“It is scary to stand here like this and talk,” she said.

"Yes, if anyone sees us, they'll think we're ghosts," he joked.

Shakun closed her mouth with her hands in a giggle. As the moonlight fell on her soft skin, Abel saw her face glitter like tiny dust of stars on the clear blue sky. He felt as though God had created the most beautiful face with his own hands and breathed life into it. Shakun felt conscious and spoke to distract him.

“Where did you and John go in the evening? You were gone for a long time,” she asked.

Abel remembered the horrible evening and grinned in disgust.

“Kavya’s house.”

“Oh." Her face fell, and she did not feel like asking anything more.

“It’s all over. Between me and her.“ Abel quickly hit the bottom line. He did not wish Shakun to assume anything.

Shakun wondered about what might have happened, but it did not matter to her anymore. She was pleased that it was finally over.

"Ok,” she said.

“Shakun… I have to tell you something important.” Abel looked serious this time. Shakun felt a tickle in her belly, and her heart pounded faster. Was he going to confess his love for her? There cannot be anything else now. She was so sure about it that she mentally planned her reactions.

“We are moving to the US. All three of us. 30th of this month.” Abel said

Shakun’s heart broke for the millionth time. 'No, no, no,’ she thought to herself and gazed into his eyes. She pretended to be calm.

“Is it? But I heard you did not want to go at all. What happened?" Shakun tried to control her anguish.

“Daddy wants all of us to go there. He is worried about Jessy. He said she will get better treatment there.” Abel wanted to add how much he will miss her but did not.

“We are also shifting to another house, on the same date.” Shakun spoke without expression.

“Mmm.. Jessy told me.” Abel said.

Both held the gate from opposite sides and looked into each other. Each wondered if they should speak their heart out or wait for the other to take the first chance. They saw love in each other's eyes, waiting to be taken. But both stood quiet. Abel felt so drawn to her. He slowly moved his hand and placed it gently on Shakun’s. Shakun gasped for breath without moving her hand away. His touch spoke all the words that she always dreamt to hear from him. She felt it magical to believe that she was finally experiencing the same flickering moments that she had always longed for. Abel moved his hand through the gaps of the gate bars and tried to touch her face. Shakun turned her face away, fearing anybody would watch them. Understanding her discomfort, Abel withdrew his hand and took a step backward from the gate.

“Sorry,” he said, feeling embarrassed.

“No, Abel. Don’t say sorry. I'm just scared. That's all. ” Shakun said, looking around. Abel waited until she calmed down and looked at him.

“Jessy will miss you a lot,” he said, totally changing the vibe of the moment.

"I will miss her too," she said.

"I think we should go back now." Abel said.

"Yes. Let's do that." Shakun agreed.

Both moved away from each other against their will and waved bye.

Abel turned to walk away when Shakun called his name. She just did not want it over yet.

"Abel," she called softly and waited for him to walk back. He came back and saw the same passion in her eyes. In a quick rush, he put his hands through the iron bars of the gate and held her face. Shakun closed her eyes, ready for whatever would happen next. Abel pulled her closer and looked at her innocent face. He felt the urge to kiss her rosy lips and slowly bent forward when they heard a door squeak.

Shakun pulled herself away and ran back in fear. She jumped up the stairs, 2 steps at a time, and reached home. She quietly sat on the floor below Winny to slow down her breath. She listened for any noise from below. There was none. Maybe somebody wanted to use the bathroom. When everything became quiet again, she slowly stood up, holding Winny, and looked towards Abel's house. She saw Abel standing near his gate with one leg bent backwards, stamping the wall. She felt sorry for running away like that. Abel stood with his head facing down when Shakun blew her last kiss for him in silence and walked back into her house.

26

October 2006—10 years later

The chill winter winds of Bengaluru made him pull up his comforter over his face.

“Good morning, hubby!” Shakun bent down, pulled the sheet down his face, and pecked him.

He looked at her with half-opened eyes and smiled.

“Today is Sunday, right?” he asked, stretching.

“That was yesterday, my darling! You have to rush now,” she reminded him and walked out.

“Oh God! It’s 7.30 already. Why didn't you wake me up earlier?“ He said, looking at his watch.

“How many times?” She asked.

Selvan turned to his side and looked into the cradle. The little boy slept with his most enchanting smile.

"What are you dreaming, my baby?" he whispered to him, stroking his chubby cheeks. The baby began to wobble with his touch. He quickly pulled up the baby blanket and gently tapped his bare chest to make him go back to sleep. He gave the cradle a gentle push and got out of bed.

Mondays were meeting days. Selvan got ready and sat for his breakfast.

Shakun placed his plate on the table. 4 idlis, chutney in a steel bowl and a fork. He gently cut them, dipped each piece into the chutney bowl, and relished them with eyes closed. She smiled and wondered how one can enjoy eating idlis with a fork. Weird.

“Today I might be late. There is a meeting on designing our company page on Facebook,” he said while washing his hands.

“What’s Facebook?” Shakun asked

“What? You don’t know yet? It’s the latest and most used social networking service that's making the world go crazy,” he said as he wore his shoes.

He was all set and picked his bag to leave.

“Do you want to reconnect with any of your forgotten friends? Try it,” he said and hugged her.

“Hmm…..interesting.” She waved goodbye and closed the door.

Shakun quickly finished the rest of the home chores, fed the baby, and sat on her bed with the day’s newspaper. From the moment Selvan mentioned reconnecting with old friends, she had been filled with curiosity. She thought of John, Jessy, and wondered most about Abel. Will she really find him on Facebook? She felt an unnecessary excitement brewing inside her with just the thought of getting in touch with him. But this time it was not the same as 10 years ago. Her heart did not beat faster. She felt no butterflies in her tummy either. She was surprised that his thought did not tickle her, and she wondered when she had stopped dreaming about her golden palace and her Prince Charming. She brought her focus back to the paper. She skipped the first few pages, which mostly focused on exaggerated stories about dirty politics or gruesome crimes committed by some psychopath. She turned the pages one by one, searching for some good news to read. And there on the international news page, she read the headlines.

“Mark Zuckerberg makes the world smaller with his FACEBOOK!!” She saw a picture of a young man smiling at her. She began reading the whole article.

‘WOW!’ she thought. ‘Will I truly find them? Jessy....Abel? Even if I do... then what?’ She asked herself

She lay down near her baby and recalled each of those wonderful days at John's house.

She decided to try. She got up and sat facing her desktop. She opened Safari and searched "Facebook.”

The internet opened to a blue page with the letter f in white, asking her to create an account. Shakun quickly made one for herself and logged in. Her eyes fell on the search bar. She quickly typed “Abel” but changed the idea and deleted it. She typed Jessy instead and pressed ‘Enter’. After a moment, she rolled her eyes when she saw the endless long list of “Jessys” that came up on the screen. She laughed out loud. There was no way she was ever going to find HER Jessy or Abel through Facebook. She sat staring at the different faces in the same name. Then it struck her mind, and she renamed Jessy to Elizabeth Jessy. The search took a few seconds, and then a face popped up in that name with Thomas added as her surname. Shakun looked closer at the picture. The lady stood in front of a snow-covered car, wearing a thick hooded jacket and cheek-hugging a man who did not look Indian. She was taller and thinner but had the same vivacious smile that Shakun recognised instantly. She clapped for herself in joy.

‘Yeaa… I got you. Jessy darling,’ she cheered. She selected the ‘Request friend’ option, which provided her with the option to send a private message. She wondered if Jessy remembered her, and just when she started to type, she got a notification from Facebook that her request was accepted. She was thrilled and opened up Jessy’s page. “Ping"—another notification came in. Jessy came on chat, and she typed, “SHAKKUUUUNNNN..is that really you??… OH MY GAAADD!!”. Shakun could actually imagine her screaming, and she laughed loudly. She unlocked the chat box and began typing.

“Hello..Jessy. How are you?”

“Am good… Thank you. How have you been? Where are you? I can't believe I found you.” Jessy typed nonstop.

"No, you didn't find me. I did.“ Shakun took the claim.

"Yes, yes..you found me...” Jessy agreed. “So tell me more.”

“I am in Bangalore now. With family.” She answered. “Where are you? Is that your husband in that photo?”

“Yes.Thomas. We are in California. We haven't returned to India since then. And yours?”

“Oh…ok. My husband’s name is Selvan," she replied.

“Selvan? Nice. John is also on Facebook. Did you find him?”

“Not yet. You are my first search,” she said.

“He is still there in that same house. Married an older woman. Has twins now." Jessy continued

“Oh..Wow…unbelievable. John with twins?? Ha ha..he will definitely teach them how to catch his chickens. It’s so strange that so many years have flown by and we lived it through without each other.”

“Yeah..true. :)”

There was a pause, and Jessy typed back.

“You are dying to know about Abel, right?” she asked directly. Shakun felt caught red-handed. She hesitated and typed,

“Ha ha…you caught me.“

“He is in New York. Married a Japanese.”

“What?...a Japanese?...” It was hard for her to accept that.

“Yea…I will tell him about you and our chat.“

“Mmm?? Will he remember?”

“Of course. We all remember those beautiful days. Even mom mentions you whenever we speak about India. Okay..it’s almost midnight here. I need to hit the bed. Catch up later. Bye.”

Before Shakun could type bye, Jessy went offline.

Shakun could not believe what just happened. She walked to her room and checked the cradle. The baby was wide awake and smiling at the fan above.

She picked him up and kissed him hard. Her eyes fell on Mark’s picture in the newspaper.

“Thank you, Mark. You have no idea what you have done.”

She sat down with the baby on her lap, and her thoughts took her back to that last day

27

April 1997: The Final Goodbye

It was just after lunch, and Shakun was in Jessy's room, helping with her last-minute packing. She sat quietly, neatly folding Jessy's clothes. Jessy's house was filled with their relatives, who had come to say goodbye and wish them safe travels. Abel's room was noisy, with all his friends laughing and joking about things that only they understood. Some ran out to buy things that Abel wanted, and some helped him pack. The chaos did not bother Shakun, as her heart thumped louder than all the noise outside.

"How did your Appa allow you to come to the airport to send us off? I am surprised." Jessy asked.

"Only because John is coming too." Shakun spoke lifelessly.

Jessy saw that Shakun was distressed about them leaving. She walked up to Shakun and hugged her tight.

"I will miss you so much, Shakun. I hope and pray that I get a friend like you there too."

Shakun looked up and smiled sadly.

"I will miss you too."

"You are also shifting tomorrow, right?" Jessy asked.

"Yes….."

"This whole street will become quiet without us. And Abel. Poor John. He would be all alone." Jessy said.

Shakun covered her face with her hands and cried. She could not yet believe that she would never see them after tonight."

Jessy hugged her tighter.

"I know you will miss Abel the most. Why can't you just tell him that you love him? There is still time. At least let me tell him."

"No Jessy. It's not required. We know."

"I don't understand what's stopping you from telling him after all that happened between you both that night at your gate. I know what happened there. I saw."

Shakun looked at her with surprise.

"What...what did you see?"

"Everything. You at the window. Abel calling you down. You both getting close. Everything."

"We just spoke because we both couldn't sleep. That's all. Nothing else happened." Shakun repeated and looked down, feeling embarrassed.

"Anyways, as you said, maybe it doesn't matter anymore. We don't even know if we will ever come back."

John knocked on the door and peeped in.

"So? Need any help, Jessy?" He asked

"Almost done. And my bestie is here to help." She looked at him and smiled.

John observed that Shakun was busy arranging the clothes when he secretly signalled Jessy to come out of the room.

Jessy understood and said

“Shakun. I need to go to the bathroom.”

Shakun nodded and continued her job.

“What?” Jessy came out and asked urgently.

“How is she? Any plans to tell him?”

"No. She says it's not necessary, and they already know it. How about my brother?” Jessy asked.

“Unbelievable. He said the same. That they know.”

“I feel awful for both of them, John.”

“And I feel proud. Just shows how deep and pure their love is. They don't even believe they need to express it."

“Hmm… I wish some miracle happens and they get together soon.” Jessy said

“Jessy,” her mom called for her.

“Ok John. Flight is at 2 a.m. We will leave by 10. Don't be late. Bye.”

“I won’t.”

The drive to the airport was quiet. All were lost in their own thoughts of the good times they had together. They reached the entry gate, and it was time for goodbyes. Shakun hugged Jessy’s mom.

“Bye, aunty. Take care, and please say my hello to uncle too,” she said.

Aunty smiled and nodded.

Shakun and Jessy hugged and kissed each other sadly before saying their goodbyes.

John took his turn to hug his friends and Aunty.

Shakun looked at Abel and controlled herself from breaking down. She walked to him and looked into his brown marble eyes for one last time. They spoke a thousand silent words, and she heard it all. Abel shook hands with Shakun and smiled. She saw the pain hidden behind his smile, and her eyes began to fill. No words were said. Not even a goodbye.

Shakun and John watched as they walked away. She waited for Abel to turn back and look at her once more. But this time she did not count. She was sure he would.

Abel walked not more than 10 steps before he turned back and winked at her. Shakun smiled back at him holding the small piece of paper that he had slipped into hers when they shook hands. While John stood there waving at them, Shakun slowly turned and opened the paper in her hand. It was a drawing of a heart, locked up with a chain around, and had the letters DG written at the centre. Her eyes scrolled down to the message written below.

"Locked you in my heart forever, My Dream Girl!!" She read. She smiled. She stood still, hanging on to that moment of infinite love.

John came and tapped her from behind.

"Let's go, Shakun," he said.

She looked at him and smiled, hiding the note in her pocket.

“Yea… let’s go… FAB!!” She said, hugging him.

That night, Shakun sat on Winny’s lap and looked up at the moon. It looked fuller and brighter, with all of her stars twinkling in cheer. ‘I am fine. Don't worry,’ she said to her nighttime friends. She placed her cheek on Winny’s chill metal and hugged her close. ‘I will miss you, Winny.’ She closed her eyes and felt the gentle breeze blowing on her face. Shakun looked down at Abel’s house. It was dark and soulless.

The next morning, while Shakun’s parents got busy with the packing, John sat next to Shakun, looking sad. Shakun had very little to pack for herself. She took John’s hand on hers.

“You will come to see me. Right?” she asked.

“Yea. And you can come too.”

“I will try not to, Fab! In fact, it all seems like God’s plan that both Abel and I had to move out of this place at the same time. He knows we both cannot continue here without each other.” She said

“Sounds dramatic. But maybe it's true. Maybe it's all for the good too.” John said.

“How can it be good for Abel and me to be apart, Fab?” Shakun asked

“Mmm.. I don't know. Maybe for your future. Perhaps God saw you both unhappy with each other in the future. Maybe he saw you both falling out of love, and he did not want that.”

“That’s not possible, Fab. I can never stop loving Abel.” Shakun said.

"Then it's better you start trying that from now on. They are not coming back, Shakun. Accept that. Just be thankful for all the beautiful moments of silent love that you both shared until now, and move on. Maybe there is someone better than Abel waiting for you."

Shakun could not believe what she heard. Someone better than Abel?

"Ammuuuu… It's time to go," her mom walked in hurriedly.

She saw John looking sad and ran to hug him.

"We will miss you so much, John. Please come and visit us whenever you can."

"Yes aunty. I will. And I am sorry that you all have to leave from here."

"It's no one's fault. Your parents and you have been so generous with us. God bless you," Amma got emotional.

Appa locked the main door and looked at it for a long time. Amma held his hand, and they walked down together. John assisted them with the suitcase and trailed behind, while Shakun stood in front of Winny, gazing out at the new world that awaited her. She ran her soft hands over Winny. She knew she'd never find another imaginary friend like her, wherever she went. She kissed Winny one last time and walked down to join her parents in the taxi. She was reminded of the day she came here a year ago. She got into the taxi and waved at John and his parents. John waved back with a smile. "I will come to see you. Don't worry," he said. Shakun smiled back and nodded her head. While the car moved, she opened her small pouch and pulled out Abel's chit of paper from amongst her few cosmetics, then read it again. She felt a sudden urge to turn behind, and there she saw him standing at his gate waving at her. She knew her heart was playing games with her again.

'Thank you, Abel, for all your love that I can never forget,' she thought to herself and smiled back.

28

Back to Bengaluru

The baby's cry brought Shakun back to the present. She put him in the cradle and swung him to sleep. She wondered if Jessy would remember to tell Abel about the chat. She did not wish to hope for anything, though.

Shakun stayed awake watching TV until late night, when Selvan silently unlocked the door and walked in smiling. Shakun remembered John's last words, "There's someone better than Abel, waiting for you." She smiled meekly, agreeing to John.

"Why are you still up, Shakun?" he asked

"Just thought to wait for you. How was the meeting?" she asked

"It went well," he said, walking in.

"Want to eat something?" she asked

We had dinner at the office. I'm too tired, Shakun. Will sleep now."

"Yeah..good night," she said and switched off the TV.

She switched off the kitchen light and walked to the bedroom. Her eyes fell on the computer, and she felt tempted to check into her Facebook account. She switched it on and waited. She did not know why she was getting so excited. She logged in and waited. She tried not to expect anything when... PING she heard the beep and saw a red dot on her message box. She felt impatient. It was from Jessy with a photo in it.

She clicked on it. There she saw the picture of Abel getting a cheek kiss from his Japanese wife. She could not believe she was actually looking at him. She stared at his face for some time. He looked different, or rather grown up. His hair looked thinner. She looked closer into his marble-brown eyes. They were still as expressive as before, and his wide, dimpled smile told her that he had a very happy life. She felt surprised that her heart did not thump any faster for him now like it did before. She felt nothing but happy for him. 'Life always gives new meaning to love,' she thought to herself as she stood up to turn off the machine, only to hear another PING. She sat down and smiled at it.